CHAINS' TRUST

Inferno's Clutch MC Book One

E.C. LAND

CONTENTS

Acknowledgments	xi
Truth	xix
Prologue	1
Chapter 1	5
Chapter 2	11
Chapter 3	18
Chapter 4	24
Chapter 5	30
Chapter 6	37
Chapter 7	43
Chapter 8	48
Chapter 9	54
Chapter 10	60
Chapter 11	66
Chapter 12	72
Chapter 13	78
Chapter 14	84
Chapter 15	90
Chapter 16	97
Chapter 17	103
Chapter 18	109
Chapter 19	116
Epilogue	122
Author's Note	127
Coming Up Next	129
Available Now	131
Coming Soon	133

Sneak Peek	135
Prologue	137
Social Media	143

Chains' Trust

This book is a work of fiction. The names, characters, places, and incidents are all products of the author's imagination and are not to be construed as real. Any resemblances to persons, organizations, events, or locales are entirely coincidental.

Chains' Trust. Copyright © 2020 by E.C. Land. All rights reserved. No part of this book may be used or reproduced in any manner whatsoever without written permission from the author, except in the case of brief quotations used in articles or reviews. For information, contact E.C. Land.

https://www.facebook.com/e.c.landauthor

Cover Design by Charli Childs, Cosmic Letterz Cover Design

Editing by Kim Lubbers

Formatting by E.C. Land

Proofreading by Jackie Ziegler

 Created with Vellum

To those who take a chance on living. Don't let the past keep you from moving forward. The mind is a powerful thing. You allow it control everything you do your heart will never get a say. Let you heart take the lead every once in a while, and you might just find your mind in agreement.

ACKNOWLEDGMENTS

My Family – I'll always be thankful toward my husband as he continues to show his support in my writing. No matter how annoying I become he lets me ramble on and on with the different things I come up with. Even sends me music when I need encouragement. My kids now are a huge part of this as I show them you can follow your dreams and shoot for the moon if you put your mind to it.

My Betas – Thank you all for being the first to read the stories as they come alive. It means the world to me. Especially when you all start to get mad. That's when I know I'm doing something right. And in doing so pushing me to keep going with all the different plots that form in my head. I'm thankful to you all for being ready and willing to read and give your input.

My Knox Publishing People – I don't know what I'd

do without you all. Your all wonderful in your own right and I wouldn't have it any other way. From encouraging me to keep going when I feel like giving up to kicking my ass when it needs it. The best thing I'm grateful for is when you listen to the different plots and scenarios I come up with. As well as the family you all have become to me.

Liz – If not for you, I don't know if I'd ever be where I am today with my writing. Thank you for always pushing me and encouraging me. Even on my worse day. Your more than just my Publisher/Boss, you're my best friend. My sister from another mister.

Diane – I couldn't be more grateful to you. You help me so much with all you take care of and have become one of my good friends. I don't know what I'd do without you considering all that you do.

Kim and Jackie – Thank you both for agreeing to work with me on all of my books. You both rock and I cannot wait to work with you both for the foreseeable future.

Playlist

The Spiral – Charlie Finley
Bullet In A Bonfire – Brantley Gilbert
Legendary – Skillet
Everglow – Starset
Hold On and Let Go – Sam Riggs
Someone You Loved – Mitchell Tenpenny
Tears Could Talk – Jelly Roll ft. Bailee Ann
Angel In Disgrace – The Raven Age
I Want Us – The Roads Below

Trigger Warning

This content is intended for mature audiences only. It contains material that may be viewed as offensive to some readers, including graphic language, dangerous and sexual situations, murder, rape, and extreme violence.

Timeline Note:

This book takes place before Blaze's Mark in the Devil's Riot MC series.

TRUTH

Life isn't fair
It never will be
People may think so
But the truth is it won't
Everyone has to fight their own war
Only it's won within
No one can see it but them
People's lives are coming to an end
As other's are being born
Is it fair
That's not for you to decide
Truth is life never is
Minds go mad
Do we shut them out or not
No one can help when it's not wanted
There's pain in everyone

Like weeds growing in the ground
It's everywhere
Truth is no one is perfect
That's life and it's not fair
Just learn to live it the way you want
Because in the end the truth is but a blur
As no one can make it be anything
Unless it's what they want it to be
Trust the truth is all you need to do
- E.C. Land

PROLOGUE

Tiny

My life has never been easy, not once from the day I took my first breath. According to my dad, I was good for nothing. Well, besides breeding to the right person. My mom died, at the hands of the man who raised me, for her sins. When I turned sixteen, I ran away. Living on the streets wasn't easy but I'd made it work. It was better than listening to the crazy that the leader of the cult would talk about.

It took me a while to make my way south. But I'd done it without spreading my legs for random men. I didn't want to be pimped out.

So, people would wonder how I ended up at the clubhouse of the Devil's Riot MC. Well I met this girl, I thought she was my friend. Told me to come to the clubhouse let the men have their way with you and you'd have the club's protection. Figured it can't be so bad.

Don't get me wrong, I'm not a slut. I did what I thought I could handle, but in the end, I didn't want to be passed around. After giving a couple blow jobs to a couple of the members of the club, I knew I couldn't hack it and confronted the president of the club, Stoney. He and Tracker understood when I explained to them why I'd come to them. They didn't turn me away like I'd thought they would.

I'd already been given the nickname of Tiny because of how short I am. Standing at no more than five foot two and weighing no more than a hundred and five pounds. Yeah you could say I'm small.

Stoney and Tracker ended up hiring me to work the bar in the clubhouse. It worked for me because then I didn't have to leave the clubhouse for anything. My room was here and thanks to the internet I was able to order clothes and whatever else I needed.

When Rachel, Stoney's ol' lady came into the picture, her and I hit it off. I started helping her with her twins, Luca and Corrine. Talk about beautiful babies. I realized helping her, what I wanted to do with my life.

I wanted to become a teacher. But you can't do that

without a college degree, and I didn't even have my high school diploma.

Then everything went to hell the night we were all attacked. Luca and Corrine were kidnapped. Rachel was beaten as well as Momma B. A few others were raped but I ended up getting the brunt of it. For reasons I don't know.

The guy, Jackal, he'd raped me, taking my virginity and leaving me scarred. Raping me wasn't enough for him though. No, he'd broken my leg and fractured my skull pretty much leaving me for dead.

It's a wonder that I'd survived, but in the end I did. However now, I'm scared to be around any of the men. I refuse to leave my room unless it's to go to the nursery for the twins.

Well that is until Victoria brought the reasons to light for the men. Stoney and Tracker gave me options of new places I could go. In the end, I asked if I could go to the Inferno's Clutch MC clubhouse. I really thought they'd say no but Stoney merely nodded sadly. I'll always remember his last words to me.

"You're family, Tiny. You might have come to us by trying to be one of the other women who come here but you're not. Don't let what happened stop you from living. Heal and know you can always come home. That's what this place is for you. Home," Stoney said, holding Rachel next to him who simply nodded her head as she smiled at me.

I'd never really had a place I called home and the fact Stoney said that made me want to cry. I wish I could have stayed, but the clubhouse scares me. All the good memories it held for me were tarnished by the evil of one man.

Sitting in the passenger seat of the truck, Shadow is taking me to Victoria's brother who said he'd take me in.

I only hope this is a good idea and that I can trust Chains.

CHAPTER ONE

Chains

"Where are we with that shipment coming in?" I ask my brothers the moment I slam the gavel down on the table.

It's been a long fuckin' week and all I want to do right now is finish church up, and have one of the strays suck me off before hitting my bed. Between the garage, the strip club, and the other few businesses we have it's been a pain in the ass recently. Tyres, Axle, and I had been stuck going through the books of all our businesses instead of getting other things done.

Seems our little accountant has been screwing up big time. I don't know if it's because she can't seem to keep her legs closed for the brothers or if it's because she's doing it on purpose. All I care about is she's fuckin' with our money and that shit ain't gonna fly.

"The shipment of girls is supposed to be coming on Thursday. Parker is expected to be there this time," Tyres says, clenching his fists.

"Good, I know the DRMC wants him. But for now, we need his sorry ass alive," I growl. I want nothing more than to hang him by his neck in the bayou and leave him to the gators.

"When we have what we want, Parker will die and it won't be pretty," Pit seethes from where he's sitting next to Tyres.

"Damn right, that fucker did enough damage to Vi. He deserves to be eaten alive by the gators. Better yet, dismembered piece by piece until there's nothing left of him," Breaker snarls. My cousins are just as protective of my little sister, Victoria, as I am.

Granted she doesn't need the protection. Vi is more than capable of taking care of herself. Unfortunately, it always comes with a price for her.

Recently her ol' man, the VP of the Devil's Riot MC, was shot and the only way for her to cope was by shutting her emotions off. She'd come down here to take out the people who raised her and Parker. I was able to soothe my sister some until Tracker got here. Didn't help Vi was pregnant and refusing to eat.

I could kill those motherfuckers for that alone. When our parents died, my aunts sold Victoria to none other than the man who'd been the governor of the state. He's another one I'd love to hang from one of my chains. Too bad no one can find him. Governor Caron was reported missing right after my sister left to go home with her ol' man and hasn't been seen since.

"Isn't that girl supposed to be showing up today?" Fuse asks.

"Yeah, what can you tell us about her?" Vi never asks anything of the club and when she'd called me about letting this woman come here, I'd immediately agreed without thinking about any of the shit we have goin' on around here.

"Tiny a/k/a Sloane Trinity Collins, twenty-one years old, was born in New York. There's not much on her except for her mother died and her father is a part of a cult moving along the east coast killing women. She ran away at the age of sixteen. There's not much else on her until about a year ago when she was admitted to the hospital and nearly died," Fuse says, sliding a file toward me.

"What put her in the hospital?" Fuse glances over at Pit before meeting my gaze. "She'd been raped and beaten. I don't know how she survived, considering the woman is no more than the size of a toothpick."

Opening the file, I'm met with an image of a beautiful woman. Her eyes alone could be mesmerizing. As I read through the report from the hospital, my blood boils at the fact this woman went through hell. According to the document she'd been in a coma for over a month.

"Vi told me Tiny needed a place to go to heal. She doesn't want us to send her to one of the safe houses we have or to Ela directly. Fury, do you think Ela would be willing to stay at the clubhouse for a few days until Tiny is settled? We don't know how she's gonna react to us," I say, slamming the file closed.

"Ela will be here," Fury mutters from where he sits at the other end of the table, next to my Uncle Ryder.

"Good, one last thing. The accountant. She's either more focused on y'alls dicks than the books or she's skimming from us. Either way we need to keep an eye on her. Keep your dicks out of her fuckin' snatch until we know what's going on. I'd hate to have to call Vi or Ray to come take care of this bitch if we don't have to." Lifting the gavel, I slam it on the table and stand up to make my way to the main room.

Scanning the bar area, I spot Dee and Tar standing near the pool tables talking with each other. I may grab them both for a little while. They can appease me together.

I've learned over the past few months to never take one of them alone. I do that and they become clingy and not wanting to leave my bed. That's a no go. I'm not about to share my bed with no bitch. Not again.

Learned that lesson the hard way and was burned in the process.

As I start to open my mouth the outside door opens and Shadow, the enforcer from the Devil's Riot MC, steps inside. Furrowing my brow, I wonder where the girl is. He was bringing her here.

Where is she?

"Yo, Shadow," Breaker calls out as he starts in his direction.

Shadow lifts his hand to stop him but still has a grin on his face.

"Where's the girl you were bringing with you?" I ask as I approach him, the strays long forgotten.

Club business always comes first.

My dick thanks me for not having to deal with the clingy bitches tonight.

"She's right here," Shadow says holding his hand behind him as he whispers something over his shoulder.

Slowly a woman steps out from behind him and fuck if she's not more beautiful in person. She's fuckin' gorgeous. Her dirty blond hair hangs well past her shoulders, face bare of makeup and I can tell she's not your typical girl.

"Hi," she whispers so softly and just with that one word I know I'd do anything to protect her.

Damn I'm fucked.

CHAPTER TWO

Tiny

Holy mother of all things hot. Can this guy be any hotter? I don't think I've ever seen a guy like him.

Okay, I lie, I've been surrounded by men like him since the moment I stepped into the Devil's Riot MC clubhouse. Only none of the guys there ever had this effect on me. At first glance at that.

"Hi," I whisper, meeting his gaze briefly when Shadow pulled me from behind him. He'd been tasked with bringing me down here, because out of all the guys he's the only one I didn't flinch around. I don't know why but for some reason he's the only one I feel I can trust.

Maybe it's the fact he's silent and barely speaks. Or it could be the way his eyes never show an ounce of pity in them like the other guys. I know they don't mean any harm but seeing that look makes me feel dirtier than I already feel.

"Hey, welcome to the Inferno's Clutch. I'm Chains the Prez of this club," Mr. Hottie says, stepping forward with his hand extended.

My first reaction is to hide behind Shadow, but I don't.

Yay, go me, that's progress, right?

"I'm Tiny," I say, reaching out to take his hand, I shake it tentatively. I'm completely freaking out on the inside about this guy touching my hand, but I'm not going to be disrespectful toward the man who has agreed to let me stay here.

"Do you have her room ready?" Shadow asks and I should be grateful he spoke up before my mind could wander to thoughts I should best not be having.

"Yeah, she's staying in the room next to mine." My eyes widen at the announcement.

I thought I'd be in a room near the other women who stay here.

"Sounds good. Let's get her shit out of the truck, I've gotta get back on the road. Shit's happenin' and I'm needed back at the clubhouse," Shadow says. I'd heard partial pieces of the conversation he'd had with Tracker about two hours ago. Something happened at

Dolly's Playhouse. I didn't get much of it, only that Blaze and Raven were involved.

"No problem. Speed," Chains calls out.

"Yeah, Prez," the guy from behind the bar says.

"You and Frame go get all of Tiny's things. Put them in her room," Chains orders never taking his eyes off me besides to give them a quick glance.

My heart feels as if it were going to come out of my chest right now.

"Tiny, I gotta hit the road as soon as they unload. You sure you're gonna be okay here?" Shadow asks. I'd swear he was acting like my big brother the way he was talking.

"She'll be good. I promised Vi nothing would happen to her and I stick to my word," Chains says before I can respond.

"I know you do Chains, but I gotta hear the words from Tiny," Shadow states.

Nodding, I meet Shadow's gaze. "I'll be okay," I murmur.

"Okay. You have all our numbers, don't be scared to call if you need anything. You're family Tiny. If you want to come home, even if just for a visit, let us know and we'll make it happen. Alright?" Shadow pulls me in for a hug, kissing the top of my head.

"I know, Shadow. I promise I'll call and text. Let me know when you get back," I say into his chest.

"You got it, kiddo." Releasing me he gives me one more look before shaking Chains' hand and heading for the door with Speed and Frame following behind him.

Turning back to face the room I meet several pairs of eyes on me. But it's Chains' gaze that ensnares me.

"Have you eaten?" Chains asks, stepping closer to me.

"I'm okay, we stopped at a burger place before hitting the Louisiana state line. I think it was What something or another. But it was one of the best burgers I've ever had. Oh, don't get me started on the tea. It was sweet just the way I like it. Which is hard to find. Sometimes you get it and it's way too sweet or it's been sitting for too long and has this weird taste to it. I don't know if that's ever happened to you. I– I'm going to shut up now," I say, realizing I was rambling.

"Come on. Since you've eaten, I'll show you to your room," Chains grins.

"Hey Prez, you gonna introduce her to the rest of us first?" a guy I'd notice standing behind him says. He's hard to miss, with how broad the guy is. Talk about muscles galore. I take a quick peek at his name on the cut he's wearing, Breaker. That's a different name I suppose, then again so is Chains.

"Let her get settled first, I'll introduce her to everyone in the morning that way Ela will be here as well," Chains says firmly as he places his hand at the bottom of my back.

"Yeah, that's probably for the best," Breaker nods in agreement. "If you need anything my room's across from the one you're staying in."

"Umm, thank you," I whisper, lifting my head to meet his gaze.

I don't know what it is about being here. Maybe it's the fact these guys don't know what's happened to me. Or it's the atmosphere. Either way I don't fear being around these men. Especially with Chains touching me. It's as if a spark shoots up my spine and I want him to do more than touch me. I want him to take me.

How that's possible only after just meeting him is beyond me? Besides I'm dirty and he would never want me.

Letting Chains show me to my room, I keep my eyes cast to the floor.

"Here we go," he murmurs, opening the door with the hand not touching me.

I step into the room and glance around. It's bare besides a bed, dresser, and nightstand with a lamp on it. Pretty basic.

"If you need anything just let me know. Speed and Frame should be bringing everything in here soon." Turning to face Chains I find him leaning against the door frame, his arms crossed over his chest.

"Thank you, I'm sure it won't take them long to grab everything. I didn't have but one box and two bags." *God can I sound more idiotic?*

Smirking, Chains straightens from the door frame. "Well, I'll leave you to it. See you at breakfast, Tiny. Tomorrow we'll go over everything and if you're ready you can start working behind the bar afterward."

"Okay great. I look forward to slinging beers again. It's better than just sitting around twiddling my thumbs." *Shut up Tiny before this guy thinks you're an idiot.*

"Good night, Tiny," he chuckles, leaving the doorway just as Speed and Frame are bringing my stuff into the room. Putting them down both men give me a once over before exiting, closing my door behind them.

Standing in the middle of my new room alone, the feelings of safety are leaving me.

"You're okay, Tiny. Just breathe. No one can hurt you," I whisper as the beginning of a panic attack creeps up.

Why was it I'd felt safe around Chains yet the moment I'm left by myself, the fear I've constantly felt seeps right back in.

Needing a distraction, I unpack my few things and take a quick shower. Leaving my hair in a towel to dry, I glance around the room looking for weak points. The only way in and out of the room is through the door or my window which are both locked. I made sure of that before getting in the shower.

Ready to fall asleep, I grab the comforter off the bed, and lay it on the floor in the corner. Lying down on the soft blanket I close my eyes. Tomorrow starts a new day and maybe a new me.

CHAPTER THREE

Chains

Over the past month, besides the day after Tiny got here, I've tried to stay clear of her. I don't know what it is about the small woman, but I'm drawn to her. All the guys like her and keep a respectful distance not wanting to scare her yet not letting her realize we knew what happened to her.

Tiny spends a lot of her time by herself in a corner when she's not working behind the bar. I also have to admit the main room and kitchen have been cleaner than I've ever seen them. I know it's because of Tiny, however, I'm not sure when she has time when a majority of her time is behind the bar.

Just because I avoided being around her didn't mean I didn't know what she was doing. I'd assigned

Frame to keep an eye on her at all times when she wasn't in her room.

Ela spends more time than usual around here talking with Tiny getting to know her. The woman is cool as shit but can be freaky as fuck sometimes too. She sees shit that none of us can comprehend but we don't fight her advice when she gives it either.

Some people call her a healer, others call her a seer. We all call her a damn snake charmer considering the way she sometimes walks around with a snake on her shoulders. Only because we can. Ela has all our respect not just as the ol' lady to one of the members but for the fact she's always there to help us when we need it.

"Yo, Prez, I gotta show you something," Fuse says coming up to me at the pool tables. Tonight's the first time I'd been out here while Tiny was working behind the bar.

"What's up?" I ask as I notice the frown on his face.

"Come take a look at something I found on the security cameras," he states, nodding his head toward the hall that leads to the room he uses for all his computer shit.

Following my brother, I tap my VP's shoulder telling him to come on as I erase all thoughts of Tiny from my mind. The club comes first and always will. "What is it you need me to see?" I ask as I enter the room. Tyres follows right behind.

"Take a look at this. I'd been wondering how everything seemed to be trashed at night yet when we get up in the morning everything is cleaned up. At first, I thought it was one of the new strays doing it but nope," Fuse says before hitting a button on the keyboard.

Focusing on the screen, I let the video feed play looking at the timestamp. This one is the night before last after two in the morning. I'm about to ask what I'm looking at when a small figure steps into the main room from the hallway leading to the patched members' rooms.

"What the fuck?" Tyres mutters.

We watch as she slowly begins to pick everything up and wipe the surfaces down. When I see her go into the kitchen only to come back out with a bucket, I'm surprised that she gets on her hands and knees to scrub the floor.

"Is this shit for real? Did Vi's ol' man know she did this shit at their club?" Tyres demands.

"I don't know but if they did, I'm sure they'd have told us," I say reassuringly as I continue to focus on the footage playing before me. "Seems we have our very own little cleaning fairy and this shit can't keep happenin'."

"You got that right; prospects seem to think they don't need to clean since the place is spotless all the damn time. I thought we were gonna have to give them bullshit jobs to keep them on their feet," Tyres chuckles.

"That's for damn sure," I growl, clenching my fist as anger seeps in. Why isn't she sleeping at that time? She doesn't have to do this shit, especially when I know for a fact, she's busting her ass throughout the day.

Stalking out of the room, I head straight for the bar and sit on a stool directly in front of where Tiny is standing, wiping down the bar top.

Glancing up she gives me a small smile. "What can I get you?"

"An explanation would be good," I say harsher than I mean to. It's not that I'm angry at her but rather the fact this has been going on for a month and we're only just now looking into it.

"Umm, I don't know what you mean, have I done something against the rules of the club?" she asks nervously, her eyes widening.

"No, you haven't done anything against the rules, Bitsy," I murmur soothingly, so that she would calm down. "What I want to know is why are you cleaning the clubhouse at two in the morning?"

"Oh, umm, I was awake so I figure I might as well clean up since the room is empty," she responds, wringing the towel in her hands.

"How come you're not sleeping at that time of the morning?" I ask furrowing my brow.

"I don't need that much sleep. I have insomnia, I guess you can say," she shrugs.

"Well do me a favor, leave some of the cleaning to the prospects and strays they've been slacking on duties because the place is constantly clean," I state before getting up and walking away. If I stayed near her any more than I already have I might do something stupid, like take her in my arms.

What the fuck is wrong with me?

Shaking my head, I go back to the pool tables where I'd been in the middle of a game with Breaker.

"Everything good?" he asks, handing me the pool stick.

"Yeah," I mutter as Dee steps up to me and slides her hands up my stomach.

"Hey, handsome, do you want me and Tar to keep you company? We haven't seen much of you and that big cock of yours lately," she purrs.

"Naw, I'm good," I say gently removing her hands from my body. "Maybe later."

"Okay, baby, we'll be waiting for you," Dee says, lifting up on her toes to kiss my cheek.

Tilting my head away from her, I avoid her lips altogether as I glare at her. She and every other stray in here knows I don't fuckin' want their lips anywhere but wrapped around my dick. It's my number one rule.

Sure, I'll grope the strays, use my hands to pleasure, but I don't ever allow them to kiss me.

Yeah, I could use them for the release they'd give me but then again, I don't think my dick will react to their fake ass tits or even them fuckin' each other. It's been this way since the moment Tiny walked through the door.

She's got my dick under a spell or some shit and that's the last thing I need right now. I swore to my sister I'd protect Tiny, but I don't need the complications of bringing her to my bed. Besides, I'm sure that's the last thing she would want anyways.

Leaning over the pool table I line up with the cue ball. Right before I take the shot my gaze lifts and connects with a beautiful pair that have haunted my dreams every night.

This has got to mean something.

Does she want me like I want her?

CHAPTER FOUR

Tiny

Deep breaths, Tiny, deep breaths. This whole situation is a mess. Being around Chains causes me to feel things I've never once felt before.

It's as if my heart is being shocked continuously as I stare at him from across the room as he hangs out with his brothers.

When one of the strays approached him, my stomach churned. Please don't let him be with her. I don't know why, all I know is Chains fascinates me and in the little bit of sleep I manage to get at night he fills my dreams. Well, him and a mixture of the nightmares I have.

Thankfully, he'd dismissed the woman and he'd gone back to playing his game of pool. The stray moved on to her next prey, but she'd kept an eye on Chains all night.

At one point I met Chains' gaze and held it for a long moment before diverting my gaze away from him.

"I suggest you stay away from Chains," the stray who Chains dismissed says, breaking the hold the man had on me as she sits on the stool in front of me.

"Excuse me?" I ask, wanting to make sure I heard her right.

"Chains, you best stay away from him. He's mine and Tar's. We're not about to share him with anyone. Not that he'd really want something as short as you," she sneers at me.

"Last I heard it's a free country and you can't belong to anyone. Besides, I think he made it clear earlier when he dismissed you like the dog in heat you are," I muttered before moving to take care of Ryder who was sitting at the other end of the bar.

Ryder, I'd learned used to be the Prez before he'd stepped down to give Chains the gavel. He'd evidently needed a change of pace and decided to go nomad for a while. He recently came back after what happened to his niece, Victoria; who is also Tracker's, the VP of the Devil's Riot MC, ol' lady.

It's strange how small the world really is when everyone seems to be connected in some way. At least I don't have to worry about any of that. Far as I know, other than my father who I escaped from there's no one else that would be looking for me. Hell, not even the vile man should be out there looking. I was nothing to him then and I always will be.

"What did you just say to me?" the stray, I can't think of her name screeches as she reaches across the bar top to grab my arm.

"You heard what I said," I say softly, not wanting to draw attention while I remove her hand from my arm.

"Bitch, you better learn your place here. You're nothing but the help," she yells, tightening her grip.

"I may work behind the bar. But at least I'm not spreading my legs for every one of these men. I bet you're so stretched out that even a bull's dong would be able to fit inside you," I snap while pinching her arm to get her to release me.

Laughter from next to her stops the woman from doing anything else. Granted, I can handle my own for the most part, I really don't want to. I may be small, but I do know how to handle my own. At least against people who aren't completely outweighing me. Well, okay, let me rephrase since a lot of people do that. I can take on this woman if need be.

"Bull's dong. That's a good one," Ryder chuckles. I hadn't even realized he'd moved from his end of the bar. "Dee, you wanna let go of Tiny's arm." The stern tone in his voice holds no barrier for argument and Dee, I guess that's her name, lets go of my arm.

"Ryder, I was just telling this bitch she couldn't talk to me or the other girls like she just spoke to me," Dee whines.

"I don't want to hear it. Honestly, I don't want to hear your voice so listen up. Tiny isn't the help here. She's a guest from another club where you are a stray. You're at the bottom of the totem pole here. I suggest you treat Tiny here with some respect because next time I'll send you out to take care of Bart," Ryder states.

"Please don't," she whimpers before darting off like a dog with its tail tucked between its legs.

"Who's Bart?" I ask in confusion when he takes a seat.

"My gator," Ryder shrugs.

"Ohhh. . . Do you really send people out there to take care of him?" I hope I never get tasked with that job.

"Someone's gotta make sure Bart gets fed," Ryder grins and I know there's a joke in that statement somewhere. I just don't know if I want to know what it is.

"What's going on over here?" I jump at the commanding tone in Chains' voice.

"Nothin', son, sit down and have a beer with me," Ryder says, patting the stool next to him.

Glancing between the two of us, Chains takes the offered seat and I grab him his beer of choice before he can ask.

"Thank you, Tiny," he murmurs, the tips of his fingers touch mine as he takes the cold bottle from my hands.

Nodding at Chains, I go back to filling orders, restocking the bar, and cleaning glasses. Dee was right about one thing; Chains wouldn't want someone like me. Not because of my height though, but rather by the fact I'm damaged.

No matter how many times I've showered I can still feel Jackal's hands on me. Smell his breath as he shoved his tongue in my mouth. Worse than the smell of his breath, I still have the marks on my skin he left. The ones with his teeth and blade.

Feeling uneasy, I excuse myself to go to my room. It's close to time for me to finish up and I need to be away from everyone right now. I'm sure they'd understand. I haven't had a day off since I started working behind the bar.

Once in my room and I have the door locked, I get in the shower. After washing my hair, scrubbing my skin raw, repeating this twice, I shut the water off and get out. I grab my towel, that I keep hung up next to the shower, as I step out.

Soon as I'm dry, I dress in a pair of sweatpants and a

tank top. This is the only time I'll allow myself to wear anything that shows more skin than a normal t-shirt. If it comes up over my stomach when I lift my arms over my head, I throw it out. I'm not about to let anyone see my scars.

Pulling my bedding off the bed, I move everything to what I've started calling my corner in the room. No one can see me from here. The bed blocks the view of me. The moment my head hits my pillow, my eyes begin to droop. I'm definitely more exhausted than I've been letting on. Which is a really bad thing, because it means only one thing.

My nightmares are going to take over.

I just hope no one hears me scream.

CHAPTER FIVE

Chains

I knew something was wrong the moment Tiny excused herself.

"What the fuck happened?" I demand as I turn to face my uncle. Ryder raised me from the moment my parents died; refusing to allow my vindictive aunts to have me after what they did to my sister.

Ryder did his best to get Victoria back, but the best he could do was gain rights to see her. The adoption was iron clad and unable to be voided all thanks to the fact it was the governor of Louisiana and his wife who not only adopted her but bought her off my aunts.

"Whatcha mean, Chains?" Ryder asks in return as he lifts his beer to his mouth.

"I'm talking about what happened with Dee and Tiny and why the hell she just walked off like she did," I growl.

"Dee was trying to stake her territory here, put her hands on Tiny when she spoke up to defend herself," Ryder shrugs

"The fuck you mean that stray put her hands on Tiny?" I snarl.

Fuck I never get this pissed over a bitch and not toward my uncle either.

"Don't worry, son, your girl took care of herself. Tiny told the little bitch that she was probably stretched out enough to take a bull's dong. Never heard anything like it, but damn if it wasn't funny. I stepped in before Dee could cause any more trouble," Ryder chuckles shaking his head.

"She's not my girl. But gotta admit that shit's funny," I state shaking my own head. Dee wants to be my ol' lady. Her and Tar. That shit won't ever happen. I don't need an ol' lady but a part of me wants to claim Tiny as mine.

Something about the woman speaks to me and I can't help it.

"Say what you want, Chains, but remember I raised you from the time your parents died. I was there when shit happened with Deanna." I can't stop myself from flinching at the mention of my childhood best friend's name. The girl I thought I'd give my heart to yet didn't. It's a good thing I hadn't because now I want nothing more than to see her dead. She's no longer the girl I saw her as but rather the enemy.

During our last two years of high school I'd noticed a change in Deanna. She'd grown harder with each day. The day we graduated she told me she was to marry another man and help run the family business.

I hadn't known at the time what that business was. Not until one night I followed Deanna home. The guy she was marrying was the very same man who killed my parents.

Delano Delancy.

I'd been hurt by the fact she'd married the vile man and cut her from my life.

Delancy is pretty much the king of Louisiana. He controls all the drugs and prostitution around here. We'd been working our way into the inner circle to take them down. The club has done some shady shit in dealing with Parker, who's the middleman for Delancy, and also the same man who my sister was supposed to marry.

I've been dying to take out Parker, but I can't. He's my in for getting closer to Delano and Deanna again. I have every intention of taking them both out eventually. It's just a matter of time. Now with Victoria protected by the Devil's Riot MC, I can maintain my focus solely on building the fire to destroy the Delancys.

"Don't talk about that bitch," I grumble.

"Not trying to, Chains, what I'm trying to get at is Tiny isn't like that cunt. She's pure of the evil our lives are filled with," Ryder says solemnly.

"That's why she'll never be mine. She doesn't need this kinda life," I state finishing my beer.

"If you say so. Just remember this, just because Deanna chose to be side by side with a man who caused you so much pain doesn't mean all women are like her. Vi isn't and neither is Tiny. My advice would be not to let your head stop what your heart wants, and I can tell you want her to be yours." With that my uncle finishes his beer and leaves me sitting there.

Lifting my beer, I chug the rest of it down and head toward my room. My uncle's words playing on a loop through my head.

He might be willing to open his heart up. But I saw what love did to those around me. I'm not about to let that happen.

Am I?

With a hand on the doorknob to my room, I glance at the closed door next to mine. Is she okay in there? Maybe I should check on her.

No. Nope, don't think about it. She's fine. Probably already asleep. She'd looked exhausted.

Sighing, I step into my room and close the door behind me.

Stripping out of my clothes, I put my gun on top of the dresser and head for the bathroom to take a shower. I turn the water on and step under the spray before it has a chance to warm up. Closing my eyes, I tilt my head back letting the water hit my face while visions of a beautiful woman fills my mind.

My dick hardens as I imagine Tiny standing bare in front of me. Her small hands run along my body while she presses her mouth against my skin.

Reaching down I stroke my dick to the vision in my head. My body's taut with need for my Bitsy and I come within minutes like a teenage boy touching himself.

Fuck.

Tiny has gotten under my skin more than I thought she had.

Finishing my shower, I step out of the stall as I reach for a towel to dry off. Wrapping the towel around my waist, I head back into my room to grab a pair of sweats out of my dresser. Just as I drop the towel and pull my sweats over my waist there's an ear-piercing scream coming from the other side of the wall.

What the fuck?

Tiny.

Grabbing my gun off the dresser and running out of the room, needing to get to my woman. I spot Breaker rushing through his own door pulling up his pants.

I don't say anything as I kick Tiny's door in. I didn't bother checking to see if it was locked or not. My main focus was getting to her.

Stepping into the room, I glance toward the bed. Finding it stripped of its bedding, I furrow my brows.

Where is she?

Whimpers can be heard from the other side of the room. Did she fall off the bed? Is that why she screamed out?

"Tiny?" I call out as I round the bed and come to a stop.

"Fuck, Prez," Breaker mutters.

On the floor lying on top of the comforter is my Bitsy.

"Looks like she's been sleeping on the floor. Bed doesn't even look slept in, there's no wrinkles in the sheets, Prez." I don't bother glancing at the bed in confirmation. Handing Breaker my gun, I silently move toward Tiny.

I'm not about to leave her in here lying on the floor like a damn dog. Crouching down I scoop Tiny up in my arms. She's so deep in her nightmare she doesn't even fight me.

"Where you takin' her?" Breaker whispers as he follows me out of Tiny's room.

"My room," I say without hesitation. It's where she belongs.

Fuck me. My uncle was right. Tiny's mine and I need to stop fighting it.

CHAPTER SIX

Tiny

Jolting awake I find myself pinned to a warm body. Panic hits me and I begin to fight my way free of the hold.

"Bitsy, calm down it's me," Chains' voice is alert as if he were fully awake and his arm tightens around me. At the realization it's Chains holding me I stop fighting him, but the panic doesn't let up. I find it hard to breathe. Like the air was sucked out of the room.

"Breathe, Bitsy. Take a deep breath," Chains says calmly, cupping my cheek.

Doing as he suggested I take a couple of breaths before tilting my head to meet Chains' gaze. As I hold his gaze it dawns on me, I'm in bed with Chains.

"Umm, why are you laying with me?" I ask in confusion.

"Bitsy, it's more like why are you laying with me? Better yet I want to know why the hell you were sleeping on the floor when you had a comfortable bed to sleep in." Oh god. Chains saw me sleeping on the floor and I'm lying in bed with him. His bed. Closing my eyes, I shake my head.

Just kill me now.

"Why would I want to kill you?" Chains asks in amusement.

Shit did I say that out loud.

"Tiny, stop talking to yourself and talk to me instead," he says, running a finger along my cheek.

"Why am I in your bed?" Opening my eyes, I'm not prepared for the intense gleam in his gaze.

"Because, baby, I didn't like bursting into your room when you were screaming bloody murder in a nightmare while sleeping on the floor," he states, the tone in his voice harsh yet gentle enough not to scare me.

"I'm sorry," I whisper, diverting my gaze embarrassed that I'd done that. This is why I don't sleep.

"Look at me," He commands, and I instantly have my eyes back on him. "You have nothing to be sorry for, Tiny. I mean nothing. Now tell me why you were sleeping on the floor."

I take a deep breath before answering. "I've never slept in a bed."

"What do you mean you've never slept in a bed?" he demands.

"I've never slept in a bed. Was never allowed to growing up and it's all I've ever known. Sleeping in the corner of a room is where I've always slept." Please don't think I'm stupid.

"Didn't you have somewhere to sleep at the DRMC clubhouse?" his brow furrows and the intensity only grows in his gaze.

"Yeah, I had a nice room with a bed, same as the one I have here but it molded into me to sleep where I always have.." I say honestly.

"Wanna explain that?"

"Not really. I don't like talking about my past," I mutter.

"You might not like to, Bitsy, but I wanna know why the hell you've never slept in a bed." The firmness in his tone is almost scary.

"Because women aren't to sleep on a bed. They're only to be in bed for one thing and that's breeding," I mutter.

Silence fills the room at my confession and Chains' gaze turns furious as he jumps off the bed like it was on fire.

"So, you sleep on the floor like a dog because you

believe the only time you should be in bed is when you're being fucked." I try to hide my wince at the way he snarls angrily, but he sees it and moves next to me. When he goes to cup my cheek, I flinch away. "Don't do that, Bitsy. I'd never hurt you. It just pisses me the fuck off that someone would treat a woman that way. I despise those types of people, baby, and I'd kill anyone who dared try to hurt you again."

Holy smokes that was the nicest thing anyone has ever said to me. But wait a minute.

"Why do you keep calling me Bitsy and baby?" I blurt before I can stop myself.

Smiling, Chains climbs all the way back up on the bed and lies next to me. When I say next to me, I mean his chest is directly against my side as he holds himself up with his arm.

"I like having my own name for you, something no one else is allowed to call you," he murmurs.

"I don't understand." I'm so confused. I don't know what's going on here.

"Don't worry, baby, I'll lead the way. Just know that from here on out, you're staying in here with me. I want you to be mine." My eyes feel as if they'll pop out of their sockets at any minute with his announcement.

"Umm, what do you mean?" He'll probably think I'm dumb as hell, but I need him to clarify this for me.

"What I mean, Bitsy, is that as of the moment I

scooped you into my arms and laid you down on my bed, you became mine. My woman, my ol' lady and I'm not about to let you go." The determination in his tone tells me the same thing his gaze does. He's totally serious right now.

Oh my god.

"What if I don't want the same thing?" I stupidly suggest.

"Is that what you want? Not to be mine?" he asks.

"I do want to be yours," I say without hesitation.

"Good, now that we have that settled I'm gonna kiss that sexy as fuck mouth of yours that I've been dreaming about for a month now," he declares right before leaning in and capturing my lips in a searing kiss like no other. I've never kissed a guy before, so I hope I'm doing it right.

I can't even count Jackal having his tongue in my mouth as a kiss. That was nothing but him forcing himself on me.

This is completely different. Earth shattering different. As Chains' tongue slips between my lips, I open my mouth to him. The way our tongues dance with each other seems to ignite something within my body.

Before I know it, Chains is breaking the kiss leaving me panting breathlessly.

"Fuck, Bitsy. That was even better than I imagined it would be," he rasps.

"You were my first," I blurt out quietly.

"First what?" Chains asks, leaning back as he stares at me with what I'd assume bewilderment.

"Kiss," I whisper.

"I'm your first kiss," he says grinning rather than asking for confirmation. "Well prepare yourself for being kissed several times a day, baby, because I think I could become addicted to you."

I don't get to respond as he leans forward again and captures my lips in yet another kiss that makes my toes curl.

Holy shit. I might be scared to death of going any further than this and I'm gonna have to say right now, I'm going to enjoy the fact Chains is kissing me.

Me the one who's covered in filth.

CHAPTER SEVEN

Chains

Over the past several weeks I've gotten to know my Bitsy. She has a funny sense of humor and gets along with all my brothers. However, she doesn't interact with them unless she's behind the bar.

Tiny hasn't come right out and said anything yet, but me and the other guys have noticed it's the only time she's comfortable joking with anyone. I've taken my time with her, wanting her to get used to being with me before taking what we have further than I already have. However, having her ass pressed against my dick makes it harder by the day.

I don't know what it is about my Bitsy but fuck if she doesn't bring out the protective side in me, especially when she freaks out when I mention taking her out of the clubhouse. I swear she ended up in a full-blown panic attack.

"Please don't make me leave the clubhouse property," she'd pleaded.

I didn't push her then for information but instead went to Fuse and asked him to look further into her past. Stupid move I'm sure. Too bad I don't give a fuck.

The woman I've claimed as mine is scared of her own shadow and refuses to leave the clubhouse to go anywhere. I need to know what's happened to her in order to help her.

Ela's been coming around more to spend time with Tiny. A couple times I've seen the woman grimace when Tiny isn't looking. If I were to ask Ela about it, I'd get the same answer she's given many times already. *'Gain her trust. Show her tenderness yet be firm. She'll talk when she's ready but prepare yourself it's not going to be easy to hear.'*

I've always hated whenever she did that. Her son, Pitch Black, said growing up with her he never got away with anything until he learned to find loopholes around her. Shit the man is still trying to find those loopholes that work without her realizing anything.

Shaking my head clear, I glance down at the paperwork on my desk. I fuckin' hate this shit. The bitch of an accountant is still skimming money off of us. Today it turned out she wasn't just distracted by all the dick but wants to play us.

"Tyres, call this bitch and have her come in," I order as I lift my head to meet my VP's gaze.

"What are we going to do with her?" he asks, his eyes lit with a fire I rarely see. There are only two things that really get him pissed, liars and thieves. Which lo and behold this little bitch is both.

Tyres and the rest of my cousins were all raised by our Uncle Ryder after what my aunts did. Those two deceitful women are the reason my cousin detests people who lie and take what doesn't belong to them.

I don't blame him for anything that happened to Vi. If anything, my cousins and I are more like brothers than anything. And those two witches are rotting in cells at the Fairy Mental Institution up in Virginia.

Weird name I know but it's just a cover for what the place really is.

A place of torture.

The director of the Institution named each level after the different regions of the underworld in Greek mythology. I believe my aunts are rotting in what is called the River of Phlegethon. In mythology it's the river of fire and at the Institution it's set up to blow fire out of the walls in random sections.

Ryder's gone there several times to make sure those

bitches are still where they're supposed to be and are miserable.

"We confront her. Ask why. If her reasons aren't good enough, we'll figure it out from there," I shrug.

Nodding, Tyres is about to say something when there's a knock on the door.

"Come in," I call out and a smile crosses my face the moment I see who it is.

My Bitsy.

"I'm sorry to bother you. I, umm, I needed to ask if someone could go to town and get a few things," she says quietly.

"Bitsy, what do you need?" I ask.

"I was doing inventory and realized I'm low on Jack and Jim. I also need a couple things for myself. I have the money to pay for it. I just need someone to go for me," she murmurs but the way her cheeks turn a bright pink, I wonder what it is she needs.

"Why don't you and I go?" I suggest and again her eyes widen as her breathing seems to become harder.

"No. Umm, I can't, I need to finish the inventory," she protests.

"We'll get a prospect to finish it," Tyres says before I can respond. "What if a couple of us go with you all. I know I need a few things from the store myself."

I could fuckin' hug my cousin right now.

"I . . . I guess that will work," she murmurs knowing

she's not going to win this battle.

I only gave in the first time because I didn't want to push too hard and scare her. With Tyres suggesting what he has, it will hopefully put her at ease.

"Bitsy, come here," I command, holding my arms open for her to come sit on my lap.

Slowly my woman makes her way over, as she gets close enough, I pull her the rest of the way into me, settling her on my lap.

"Why do you feel scared about leaving the clubhouse?" I ask.

Tiny glances from me to Tyres then focuses back on me.

"Whatever it is, you can say in front of him. He's not only my VP, but he's my cousin." I say firmly. I'm learning when it comes to Bitsy you have to use firm tones with her. However, when someone yells, she flinches and steps back as far as she can.

"B–Because I'm scared. I don't want to be taken. I– If he finds me, he'll take me and make an example of me." The fear in her voice sends my protective instincts into overdrive.

"Who?" I demand.

"My father and his men," she whispers so quietly I almost don't hear her.

Fuckin' hell if it's not one thing it's another and now I'll have to make sure everyone is on high alert.

CHAPTER EIGHT

Tiny

Confessing my greatest fear almost feels like a weight off my shoulders.

Almost.

Sure, it's not the only thing that I fear. I fear Jackal or someone like him will get ahold of me again and do what he did to me.

Fear consumes me with everything that I do. I guess you can call me a scared pansy or whatnot.

"How about we make it a run? All of us go for a ride and then we'll stop long enough for you to get what you need from the store." My heart stops at the caring thoughtfulness of Chains. He's been nothing but tender with me since we started whatever we are.

I wish I knew what we were exactly. I don't want to assume anything, but I also don't want to ask.

"Okay," I murmur in agreement.

"Good, Tyres, go let the brothers who are here know we're going for a run. Have a prospect take a cage and meet us in town. We'll put whatever we get in there," he orders his VP, while running a hand along my spine.

Tingling sensations shoot through my body as I savor his touch.

"You got it, Prez. When do you want to leave?" Tyres asks.

"Thirty-minutes," Chains says, glancing in his VP's direction briefly.

The moment Tyres leaves us alone, Chains guides my movements until I'm straddling his lap.

"Now that we're alone, I want to get a couple things straight, Bitsy," he says calmly. I don't respond as the all-knowing fear starts to creep in. Did I do something wrong? "First things first. When it comes to going out of this clubhouse, you have nothing to fuckin' worry about. You want to go to the store a prospect will go with you to make sure you're safe. Want to go for a fuckin' walk? Go for it. If I can't go with you then same thing, a prospect or even one of my brothers will go with you.

"Second thing, if the sperm donor who raised you

even tries to come close to you, he'll get a nice bullet between the eyes. Better yet, I'll chain him up down in the bayou and let the gators have him. Bart's not the only gator around here.

"Last thing, you have nothing to fear from any of my brothers. They'd take a bullet before ever hurting you so don't think the only time you can laugh and joke with them is when you're behind the bar. You're mine, Bitsy. I won't have anyone causing you any form of fear."

I should have realized he'd figure out that was the only time I really interacted with the other club members. It's stupid of me to think that I could hide something as simple as hiding my fear from Chains. He's the type of man who can sense someone's fear.

"Okay," I finally murmur.

"Good," he grins lifting a hand from my waist to grip my hair at the back of my head in order to pull me closer to him for a mouthwatering kiss.

God knows Chains can kiss and I've come to love having his mouth on mine. It's almost like when we're connected like this, he's a part of me. Since the first kiss, I've become more and more comfortable with him and I want to go further than just kissing.

I know he wants more as well, considering the hardness growing between us. Feeling bold, I grind myself against him, rubbing my core against Chains' hardness.

As Chains breaks the kiss, I moan in protest and open my eyes. Hell, I was so consumed by him I didn't even realize I'd closed them. Meeting his gaze, I'm transfixed by the lust in them.

"Bitsy, when we get back tonight you're mine," he growls, releasing the grip on my hair he moves both hands to my waist to hold me in place. "I've been waiting for you to show me you were ready, and you have some shitty timing. But tonight, baby, when we get back from our little shopping trip, I'm officially making you mine."

I never knew such simple words could cause me to feel the things that I am right now. However, with Chains, he has me wanting so much more.

"Now let's get out of here before we skip the shopping trip all together," he states, patting my ass.

"Maybe we should," I murmur, clutching his shirt in my hands.

"I'm sure you think so, baby, but you said you need some things so we're goin'." Sighing I know I'm not getting out of this. Not even for the better joys of pleasure.

Damnit.

"Fine," I pout as I climb off his lap.

"It'll be fine, Bitsy, you'll see," Chains says with a firmness in his tone that I find soothing.

Nodding, I glance down at the floor becoming

nervous this time rather than the fear that took hold earlier.

Here we go. I'm about to plunge into the deep end by doing something I haven't done in years.

Other than the ride down from the Devil's Riot MC, and my stay at the hospital, I haven't left either club once stepping inside. No reason to when all I want to do is hide in the shadows and never be found.

With my hand firmly in Chains' he guides the way from his office to the main room of the clubhouse. As we step in the room, I find it bare of anyone. I follow behind Chains as he guides me toward the front door.

"Shouldn't I go grab my money?" I ask before he opens the door.

"Nope," he states pulling the door open stepping through.

Sucking in a breath, I hold it as I step through as well.

Once outside, I glance up to meet his gaze.

"How am I going to get everything that I need without it?" I ask already knowing his answer.

"Bitsy, when you and I go off together anywhere I handle the bill," he says.

"But I can pay for my own things," I protest.

"Not saying you can't but when we're going anywhere together, you let your ol' man take care of it." He doesn't give me a chance to argue anymore about the fact by pulling me over to a gorgeous slick motorcycle. Shades of grays and blacks mixing together to create beauty stands in front of me as he climbs on. Looking closer at the fuel tank the two colors swirling together actually look like chains blended into the paint.

Holy shit that is awesome!

"Your bike is beautiful," I say, gaining a chuckle from him and several others I hadn't even bother to realize were around us.

"Baby, get on the bike and let's get out of here before you make me change my mind," he commands as he holds a hand out for me to take.

"And that's a bad thing," I smile feeling a little ballsy.

"Bitsy, get on the fuckin' bike now," Chains growls, but his gaze holds a sparkle of lust in them that I can't wait to see more of.

CHAPTER NINE

Chains

Fuck me, if watching my Bitsy as she takes in the French Quarter isn't something to see I don't know what is. What I do know is my cock is on the verge of bursting out of my fuckin' jeans right now.

"Tiny looks like she's a kid in the candy store," Breaker says from next to me as we watch her glancing in the windows of the different shops we pass by. However, I'd noticed she'd yet to go in any of them.

"Yeah, she does," I grin, not taking my gaze off my woman. It may be daylight right now, but we know the dangers that surround us. If a woman catches the wrong attention out here, she could easily be scooped up and never seen again. I'm not about to have that happen to my Bitsy.

"You really like her, huh?" Breaker murmurs.

"She's the one I've been waiting for. I remember my dad telling me when you find the one who speaks to your soul you'll know. Fight if you want but in the end your heart will take you where it's meant to be," I say, repeating his words as they pop to the front of my mind.

"Good. Your dad knew what he was talking about and if you didn't snag that woman up, I definitely would have. She's not a stray and deserves to be treated like a queen," Breaker grins as I narrow my gaze on him.

"Don't ever mention you snagging my ol' lady again, brother," I growl. Love him and the rest of my brothers but I don't want to ever think about any of them wanting to be with Tiny. She's mine and that's never gonna change.

Deciding she needed to finally stop window shopping and go inside. I step up behind my Bitsy and wrap my arms around her waist to guide her into the store we were currently standing in front of. I internally groan realizing it's a bookstore but Tiny tilts her head up and grins at me. Guess she must love books.

Shit. I need to learn more about her other than what I already know. Not knowing the simplest thing like this is fucked up. Then again, we have the rest of our lives, if I have it my way, to learn every little detail about each other.

Tiny roams the aisles of shelves for a good five minutes or so before stopping and picking up a book to read the back of it.

"Find one you want?" I ask as I stand directly behind her and wrap my arms around her. She stiffens at first but almost immediately relaxes her body against mine.

"Umm, yeah," she whispers but she goes to put it back. Reaching out I grab the book from her and turn it so that I can see the front.

I frown when I realize the book isn't just some romance bullshit like my sister and Raven read.

"Why do you want a *Study Guide for a GED* book?" I ask, holding the book up in my hand.

Blushing, Tiny looks to the floor. "Because I never finished school," she murmurs so softly I barely hear her.

"Bitsy, look at me baby," I command, and her gaze snaps up to mine. "Why didn't you finish school?" I know the answer just by the look in her eyes before she shakes her head in response. She didn't get to because she'd run from home and has been in hiding ever since and that shit's gonna stop. Tiny isn't gonna hide from the world anymore.

Nodding, I take my ol' lady in my arms, still holding

the heavy book in one hand. "Don't worry, baby. We will get you set up so you can go to school if that is what you want. I'll have Fuse set you up with online classes. But listen to me now. Just because you didn't finish school doesn't mean you're stupid or anything else. Okay?"

"Thank you." With a slight smile on her face she leans further into my chest, laying her head against me.

"Nothing to thank me for, Bitsy. You're my ol' lady and I'll do what I have to, to make you happy," I murmur, lifting a hand to cup her chin in order to bring her gaze to meet mine.

As I hold her gaze, I tilt my head down to brush my lips against hers gently.

"Get a room, Prez, it's a bookstore for God's sake," Brake chuckles.

"Fuck you, Brake," I mutter, irritated at the interruption.

Chuckling, Brake moves closer to us, "Sorry to break up y'alls moment but thought you'd want to know Delancy has been spotted."

Stiffening, I release my grip on Tiny's chin and turn my attention to my brother. "Which one?" I demand.

"Deanna," he says, and my anger takes hold.

"Come on let's get out of here," I command, tossing the book back on the shelf. Tiny won't be needing that. I'll make sure she gets her High School

Diploma rather than a GED. She deserves it and I won't settle for less.

Tiny follows without a word and for that I'm thankful. I don't think I could handle answering her questions right now. Not when I need to make sure Deanna doesn't see her. If she does, I'm sure she'll become a target. For several reasons. One: Tiny's beautiful. Two: She fits the type they like to snatch up. Three: Deanna is a jealous bitch and will take Tiny for herself if she knows that she's mine.

Deanna may be married to Delano but she's a vindictive bitch when it comes to things she can't have. It's because of her parents she had to marry her husband rather than getting to be with me. For that she's hated the fact I didn't fight for her. My thoughts on it were she didn't fight for me knowing that her husband, who's at least fifteen years older than her, killed my parents.

I never should have brought Tiny to the French Quarter knowing there would be a risk of this but fuck Tiny deserves to come here.

"Umm, Chains," Tiny says as we make it to my bike.

"What's wrong, Bitsy?" I ask while I grab her helmet to hand her.

"I umm, I didn't get a chance to go into the store that I needed to," she says, a blush tinting her cheeks.

Frowning, I glanced around the area to make sure

all my brothers were preparing to follow me. And also, to make sure none of Delancy's men were watching.

"I needed to go somewhere like Wal-Mart or Target," she murmurs.

Fuck, I should have asked her what store she needed to go to before we left the clubhouse.

Damnit.

"Alright, baby, I'll take you there let's get out of the French Quarter first though okay?" I suggest, trying not to show my annoyance.

It's not her I'm annoyed with, it's myself.

Actually no. It's the fact Deanna had to ruin our fun by showing up today.

Normally I don't give a rat's ass, but I have to think about Tiny now. I need to make sure she stays safe no matter what. I refuse to let Deanna or Delano get their filthy hands on her.

CHAPTER TEN

Tiny

Since leaving the French Quarter, Chains has been in a sour mood.

I don't know who this Deanna Delancy person is but I'm guessing, with the way he's been acting, she's not someone he likes. I want to ask him about it, but it isn't my place.

Honestly, I really don't know what my place is here. Chains says I'm his ol' lady but why would he want someone damaged like me. Not when he could have any woman he wanted.

Now as he follows me through the store, I begin to feel completely self-conscious with myself. I barely had clothes and such when I moved here along with personal products. It was almost my time of the month and I ran out of what I had the last time which had been right after moving here.

Going down the personal care aisle, I pick up a cheap thing of shampoo and conditioner before I move down further toward the soap to pick up the least expensive one. I make my way closer to the personal products without giving Chains a glance. Picking up what I need, I glimpse the condoms sitting on the shelf further down and wonder if maybe I should grab some.

As I stop in front of them, Chains finally speaks up. "What are you doing, Bitsy?" he demands.

"Umm, I didn't know if I should pick up a set." I murmur, glancing up at him.

"Baby, don't need' em," he growls.

"But . . ." I stop myself from saying anything else. I guess my thoughts of us earlier today are not happening. Or he's changed his mind.

"Don't need' em. Got some already. You done in here?" he mutters as he grabs hold of my hand. Turning me to him, Chains wraps both arms around me.

Instead of answering out loud, I nod my head in response.

"Bitsy, don't look upset. I'm not saying this shit to upset you. I'm saying it for the fact I don't need my ol' lady staring at condoms like she's trying to figure out what size to get for me. My dick is hard as fuck now thinking of being inside you. Following you around in here is torture as I keep staring at your ass."

Well okay. I guess that's a good thing.

I do my best to give him a sincere smile, granted I'm still very self-conscious right now. I mean I'm the stupid one for thinking we would need protection.

"What's with the fake smile?" he asks softly as he steps away.

Shaking my head, I look at the floor. "It's not fake. I've got everything I needed."

"Tiny," he says as he grabs my arm. "Don't lie to me."

"I'm not lying," I whisper.

"Yeah, you are. Now tell me," he commands.

"I just should have known you'd already have condoms. I shouldn't have assumed we needed them. I'm stupid to have thought otherwise." I have to take a sharp breath to keep tears from forming in my eyes.

"Bitsy, you ever call yourself stupid again, I'll make sure you aren't able to sit for a week. As for the condoms, you were thinking of protecting yourself. Which is a fuckin' good thing, but remember it's my job to protect you," he murmurs pulling me back into him. "Now let's check out and get the fuck out of here."

I nod in agreement as I'm unable to respond to

him. The thought of having his spanking shouldn't send a thrill through me but it does.

As we check out Chains takes a look at some of the things I'd picked up from the clothing department.

"Damn, I wish I'd paid more attention to this shit as you were picking it out, Bitsy," he mutters as he reaches down to adjust himself.

I'll take that as him approving of my boy shorts and thongs. I'd need more of those along with some tank tops, shorts, and I'd found a hoodie on clearance that I really wanted. Since I normally never have money, I stick to marked down prices or thrift stores. I've found whenever I can afford it sweatshirts and hoodies are the only things I'll splurge more than fifteen dollars on.

"Your total is $57.86," The cashier's voice hauls me out of my thoughts and I open my mouth to say I'd like to put some items back because I of course didn't add everything up, Chains hands her the cash for my purchase.

"Here ya go," he says as he grabs hold of the bags.

A moment later the cashier hands Chains his change. "Have a good day," she says all but purring as she winks at him.

"I plan on it," he grins putting an arm around my shoulders. "Come on, let's get out of here. We have some unfinished business, Bitsy. I can't wait to have you model them undergarments for me when we get back to the clubhouse."

"Okay." Is all I can think to say at his announcement. I might not be pretty, but Chains definitely has a way of making me feel that way. And at least for now I'm good enough for him.

By the time we got back to the clubhouse all the brothers of the club were ready to party and have a good time. As I head inside, I start to go behind the bar; however, Chains stops me.

"You're not working tonight," he murmurs as he pulls me out of the main room and down the hall toward his room. "Besides, Bitsy, we have some unfinished business to take care of." The grin he gives me sends a shiver through my body and my core aches with need. After being on the back of his motorcycle, feeling the vibrations of the motor between my legs I can hardly wait.

Catcalls and whistles follow us as Chains calls out over his shoulder to leave him the fuck alone for the rest of the night. He also told them they'd be having church tomorrow at noon.

Stepping into the room, my nerves are a wreck as

anticipation fills me. Will he like what I look like under my clothes? Scars and all.

Chains locks the door behind him sealing us in the room. He steps around me as he removes his cut and tosses it on the chair at his desk. His gun holster and knife follow. The last thing he does is empty his pockets, tossing his wallet, keys, and phone on to the desk.

Finally, he turns his attention to me. My breath catches in my throat at the lust filling his gaze. "I'm gonna hop in the shower, wanna join me?" he asks, never once taking his gaze from mine.

This is it. This is the moment where everything will change between us. I trust him more than anyone else and that scares me. Because I'm sure once he sees my body, he'll throw me away.

Taking a deep breath, I nod my head as I lift my shirt above my head. Might as well have him prove me wrong before I give him anything else.

My heart to be exact. If he takes my body, I will never be able to walk away from him.

He'll own me body, heart, and soul.

I just know it.

CHAPTER ELEVEN

Chains

The moment Tiny took her shirt off, I didn't give her a chance to shy away. Instead I erased the handful of steps between the two of us and pulled her into my arms.

"You're beautiful, baby," I murmur, running my hands down her spine. Tiny doesn't say anything in response and I can tell she's nervous. Moving my hands from behind her back, I grab hold of hers and pull her into the bathroom with me.

I release her hands in order to turn the shower on. Once I have the water warming up, I meet Tiny's gaze and hold it while taking my time to remove her bra from her body. Soon as it falls to the floor, I finally look down to see her perky tits with little rose buds for nipples.

"Fuckin' beautiful, Bitsy," I murmur, using a hand to cup one of her small breasts.

I brush my thumb across her nipple causing Tiny to moan. "You like that, baby?" I ask.

"Yes," she moans when I do it again.

"Good. I intend to do a lot more to you before the night's over with," I say.

"Chains," she murmurs, and I release her breast to cup her chin.

"Bitsy, when we're alone I'm not Chains to you. The only name I want you screaming when I'm fuckin' you is Darren. You're not some stray and I'll never treat you like one. Got me?" My Bitsy's eyes widen with each word I say.

Tiny seems to want to say something, but instead she nods her head in response.

"Need the words, baby," I demand.

"Okay, Darren," she whispers and it's my undoing.

Sliding my hands down her body, I unbutton her jeans and slip them over her small rounded cheeks. Everything about my woman is small. I swear it's not natural for her to be so petite, but she is and there's nothing I can do about it.

As Tiny steps out of the legs of her jeans, I step back enough to enjoy the sight of her body while stripping out of my own clothes. Tiny's gaze roams my body with each article I remove. Granted she's seen me in boxers, she has yet to see all of me.

A gasp escapes in a breath as her eyes seem to look like they're about to pop out of their sockets when I drop my boxers.

"Don't be scared of it, baby. It's not gonna bite you," I chuckle as I fist my dick, giving it a stroke for her view.

"That isn't going to fit," she blurts out.

"Sure, it will. But I'm not worried about that right now. First, we're going to enjoy a shower while exploring each other's bodies." I'm sure I sound like a fuckin' pussy right now. I honestly don't give a flying fuck. My woman deserves to feel special.

Taking Tiny's hand, I guide her into the shower, making sure to check the water isn't scalding hot. I'm not trying to burn her delicate skin.

"Ummm, since you don't want me calling you Chains when we're alone, can you not call me Tiny?" she asks.

"Why don't you want to be called Tiny? And if I might point out I call you Bitsy and baby and I'm not, not going to call you those. It's my own personal nicknames for you," I grin.

"It's not that I mind it. But I'd kinda like for you to at least use my real name. No one ever has. Not even when I was growing up. It was always "girl", get over here." Anger on her behalf starts to seep in, however I force it back for now.

"Okay, baby, I can do that. What's your first name?" I ask though I already know it. I just don't want her to know I do. She doesn't need to know I've got a file on her.

"What you didn't have Fuse do a check on me?" she asks, jokingly.

Well fuck me. I'm not going to lie to her and say I didn't.

"Yeah, Bitsy. I did. You've been around a club. You know we don't let anyone in without it. But doesn't mean I don't want to hear you tell me your real name. I don't care about a damn thing that I've read about you. I want to always hear it from you even if I already know." Tiny stiffens as she takes in my words.

"You know, don't you?" she states rather than asks. Her gaze drops to the floor.

"Look at me," I command softly, and she does so with tears filling her eyes. "Yeah, I know what that fucker did to you. I also know what Stoney and Tracker told me. They told me how you came to the clubhouse agreeing to be a clubwhore but I also know you didn't fuck anyone. Stoney told me about the fact you did one thing and then decided that wasn't for you, so you talked to him and Tracker and they hired you to work for them instead.

"I already told you, I don't see you as a stray and when you came to this clubhouse you didn't come as one. You were sent here to heal and feel protected. Well, Bitsy, I intend to keep on protecting you and always making sure you feel safe. Trust me when I say this because I don't say it lightly. The moment I saw you step around Shadow, I knew you were meant to be mine. I fuckin' love you woman."

Lifting a hand to cup the side of her face, I stroke the tears away from her cheeks. "Don't cry, baby. It guts me seeing you in tears."

"I'm sorry. I–I just was so scared that if you knew you wouldn't want me. I love you too, Darren, and that scares the hell out of me." I pull her into me wanting to comfort her.

"Nothing could keep me from wanting you. We're made for each other and nothing will ever change that, Sloane," I state making sure to use her first name, not giving a damn she doesn't tell me first. Not anymore.

Her gaze holds mine for long moments before she lifts herself up on her toes. I lean down to meet her halfway, crashing my mouth to hers. Cupping her ass in my hands, I lift her up into my arms as she wraps her legs around my waist.

Now this is what I envisioned when we stepped in

here but I'm glad we got that shit out of the way. Tiny doesn't need to be worrying about if I really want her or not.

By her making the first move after that little heart to heart, I know she trusts me more now than ever.

CHAPTER TWELVE

Tiny

Kissing Chains right now is like a weight has been lifted. After his admission, I know without a doubt I want him more than anything.

Moaning into him, I grip his hair while rubbing myself against his dick. The sensations it causes in my body are almost unbearable. I need more of him.

A groan vibrates from his mouth and it spurs me on.

I still say he's not going to fit, but I can't stop myself grinding against him sending jolts of pleasure through my body.

When Chains breaks our kiss, I start to protest but he moves to trail kisses down my jaw to my neck.

"Darren," I sigh, wanting so much more.

"Don't worry, Bitsy, I know what you need. Just enjoy the pleasure I give you," he commands, his voice deep with arousal.

I mumble in agreement as I tilt my head to the side giving him even more access.

"That's right, baby, just relax and enjoy my mouth on you," he murmurs then I feel movement and we're stepping out of the shower soaking wet.

"Ummm."

"It's alright. We'll be needing another shower when I'm done with you," Chains declares, and I can't help but giggle.

"Laugh now, Sloane, cause in a couple minutes, you'll be screaming my name," he rasps, his gaze meeting mine as he lays me across the bed.

"You should know I've never done this. Well you know besides . . ." I let my words trail off not wanting to ruin any of this for either of us.

"Sloane, baby, don't think of any of that negative bullshit. I don't give a fuck about anything but making you come all damn night," he says pressing kisses along my skin until he has my legs braced on his shoulders.

Bracing myself up on my elbows, I meet Chains' gaze as he grins before lowering his head. With a swipe of his tongue through my slit, I immediately moan in pleasure. I've never felt anything good. Not with how good it feels to have his tongue licking me the way it is.

When he presses a finger inside my pussy, I cry in pleasure from the intrusion.

My back arches when Chains nips at my clit.

"Darren," I moan, feeling myself growing closer to orgasm.

"That's right, baby, let it go. I want to taste you as you fuckin' come for me," he growls, removing his finger and replacing it with his mouth. Thrusting his tongue into me and I do just as he orders.

I come, screaming his name.

Chains doesn't give me a chance to come down from the pleasure induced high he'd just given me. No, he shoots up to a kneeling position, my legs now braced in the crook of his arms.

Meeting his gaze, my breath catches in my chest at the sight of how gorgeous he is hovering over me. His eyes gleaming with lust and love combined.

"Time to officially make you mine, Sloane. After this I'm never fuckin' letting you go," he growls, reaching into the side table he grabs a condom.

He quickly rolls the thin latex over his dick and I already sense a small pang of regret that I won't feel him skin on skin.

Soon as he has the condom in place, Chains lines up his dick with my entrance and slowly thrusts into me.

"Darren," I moan, wanting more but feeling so full at the same time.

"I know, baby. I'm going slow right now so you can adjust to my dick," he grinds out as he pushes further.

Inch by inch he continues to fill me until he's all the way inside. Groaning, he doesn't move. It's as if he's doing his best to treat this as if it were indeed my first time. "You're fuckin' tight as hell, Bitsy."

Moaning in response, I move my hips needing more from him. To feel him moving inside me. I want to have what I have dreamed about with him. For him to overtake my body with his and dominate me with pleasure.

Chuckling, Chains slides all the way out causing me to groan in protest. "You want my dick, baby?"

"Yes," I murmur, nodding my head enthusiastically.

"I don't think you do." The way he slides the tip of his dick along my entrance is maddening.

"I do, Darren. Please give it to me. Make this the only experience I ever remember," I beg and Chains' control seems to snap.

"Sloane, when I'm done with you tonight you won't even remember anyone else ever touching your body. Good or bad. You'll only know my touch. My kiss," He growls, slamming all the way home with each word. Punctuating his meaning.

When he finishes his declaration, Chains leans forward to capture my mouth in a searing kiss as he grips my hips tighter and his thrusts become deeper with this angle. I wrap my arms around his neck as I grow closer to the edge of an orgasm building within me ready to explode at any moment.

"I'm gonna come," I pant when Chains breaks the kiss. My nails are digging into his skin the more he pounds into me.

"Then come, baby. Tighten that pussy more than it already is and drench my dick." Oh, shit the way his voice drops to a baritone does something to me and I can't keep myself from doing what he commands.

Screaming his name, my vision blurs as I come. My orgasm seems to go forever when Chains reaches between us and pinches my clit sending me sailing even higher.

Long moments later Chains growls my name as he joins me in oblivion.

"Fuckin' hell, Bitsy," Chains grunts, his dick still twitching inside me as he braces himself on his elbows. "We're going all damn night and every night from now on. Or until I fuckin' die of being buried in your tight pussy."

A giggle escapes me at his announcement.

"Just think your headstone could read dead by TP," I laugh.

"TP?" he asks, arching a brow.

"Tight Pussy." He chuckles when I explain the abbreviation.

"Shit, that's funny, baby," Chains states, shaking his head as he pulls out of me causing me to groan in protest. "Don't worry. I'm not done with you. Remember we're fuckin' all damn night."

"I don't know if I can handle anymore," I murmur.

"Oh, you can handle it, I promise you that," he grins as he removes the condom and ties it.

Leaning to the side of the bed, he reaches into the draw for another one and lays it on the bed next to me.

"We'll use this one again in a few minutes. First, I want you to ride my face," he says, huskily as he rolls us until I'm sitting on his chest.

Starting to feel nervous, I try to slide down his body. "I, um, I don't know how," I confess when he grabs hold of my waist.

Grinning from ear to ear, Chains moves me to where he wants me. Directly over his face. "I'll teach you, Bitsy. I'll show you everything you need to know and more," he says right before he does just that, making my throat raw from screaming his name over and over throughout the night.

CHAPTER THIRTEEN

Chains

Sitting in my chair at the table where our club holds church, I inwardly groan as I thank the caffeine gods for the coffee in my hand. Exhausted from last night's events.

Well more like events that lasted until the sun came up this morning.

I have created a monster out of my woman and fuck if I'm going to complain. Last night I fucked my woman every way I could think of and then some. I never knew a woman to be as flexible as she is, and the positions I'd put her in makes me want to find one of those *Kamasutra* books.

"Prez, you're looking a little rough today," my VP, Tyres, chuckles.

"Fuck you," I grumble lifting my coffee cup to my lips, needing the caffeine more than ever right now.

Today, I'd called church for my brothers and I to discuss shipments coming up and to figure out a game plan with the Delancy's. I'm fuckin' done waiting for the right moment. Or for Parker. It's time they all died.

"Fuse, what do you have for me on Delancy and Parker?" I demand as I down more of my coffee.

"Besides, Deanna being spotted yesterday in the French Quarter neither Delano, nor Parker have been seen lately," Fuse states as he shakes his head. A lot of people don't get our brother. Considering the tattoos that coat his body he looks like the rest of us; however, Fuse is different which is what makes him fuckin' good at what he does.

Due to something to do with his nervous system, he has a sensory issue that affects how his mind works. No one outside of the members of the club know about it and that's the way we want to keep it. It's no one else's business what our brother deals with.

"Are our eyes still working at their place?" Tyres asks.

"Yep. However, nothing has been going on out of the normal sex fest they always seem to be having. The parties are constant," Fuse sneers. "Those people are masochists. Every last one of those parties they string a woman up in the middle of the room and Deanna or

Delano will take a whip to the woman. The last one looked as if she died from the way her head slumped over to the side when the cord wrapped around her throat."

"Shit, that's fucked up," Breaker mutters.

"You're telling me. I had to watch that shit with Fuse," Brake grumbles.

"Look, I know we had planned to get into the inner circle in order to take them out; however, I think we need to change our game plan. I'm not going to put Tiny at risk of Deanna's wrath. We all know what that bitch will do to my ol' lady if she finds out about her," I state.

"I agree," Ryder says from the other end of the table. "I've waited for fuckin' years to take Delancy out. He took my brother and sister-in-law out, all because Chains' mom wouldn't leave her ol' man for him. Deanna ended up marrying the fucker so she wouldn't lose her money. Now she's as crazy as that fucker. If not more so."

"I'd say she's worse. I feel for the children that she's had with Delano," Tyres mutters.

"They'd be better off without either of their parents at this point," I grunt.

"What do you think about calling Vi and Ray home? Let them help us in getting this organized. You know Tracker wants Parker for himself," Fury suggests from his place next to my uncle. Glancing at him, I know he's trying to tell me something. Probably something Ela has said.

"I don't know," I say, leaning back in my chair. I don't want to bring my little sister into this bullshit. She's finally happy and doesn't want to be Silent Night anymore unless she absolutely has to. Besides that, my nephew was born not too long ago premature thanks to a bombing. I don't want to put her in a predicament that would take her away from her son. Granted, Tracker wouldn't let that happen anyway. I respect the man for who he is and the love he clearly has for Vi.

"I know you don't want to call her, but Vi and Ray both have talents that can help us do what we're going to want to do. What we'd originally wanted to do can be done but we'd have to push everything up on the timetable. Meaning, we'll need their help," Ryder states.

"What about Harlow?" Pitch Black proposes.

"Fuck no," Lynch, Harlow's brother, snarls from next to his cousin. "Don't bring Harlow back here. It won't do any good."

"I don't know about that," Fury says. "It might actually do Harlow some good coming here."

"No, my sister has been through enough fuckin'

shit. She doesn't need to come back here and deal with more," he mutters.

"I have to agree with Lynch. Vi and Harlow have both been through enough bullshit in their lives. They don't need to be brought into our situation here. Besides, we don't need them to do our jobs. We've been handling our own shit for a long time now," I say, scanning the room making sure to meet each of my brothers' gazes. "We have a code, brothers. *Never harm those we love. Never bring the innocent in the middle. Never let our backs be put to the wall.* Those women are innocents from now on. We can do this ourselves."

Nods of agreement fill the room as every one of my brothers bangs a fist on the table. Lifting my gaze to my uncle, I see him grinning at me as if he'd been testing me.

Fucker.

Love him but fuck if he can be a pain in my ass. Then again, he technically should still be the Prez of our club not me. But he refuses to take it back wanting to just sit back and be a member of the club rather than deal with the headaches I do.

"Then what do you want to do, Prez," he says nodding his head in approval.

"Here's what I'm thinking," I grin as I start to go over details of a plan I'd been working on since the first time I realized Tiny was goin' to be mine.

I refuse to let anyone hurt my woman and I'll kill anyone who stands to harm her or my club. As I said earlier. *Never harm those we love. Never bring the innocent in the middle. Never let our backs be put to the wall.* And I intend to make sure that nothing happens.

CHAPTER FOURTEEN

Tiny

Over the past month, since Chains and I took our relationship to the next level, I've never felt so many emotions. Throughout the day he seems to be so distracted, barely speaking to me or isn't here period.

At night is a different story. When he comes into the room, the first thing he does is strip out of his clothes and sinks deep into me. Afterward, Chains holds me to him like nothing was going on. I may not be that smart, but I know something is going on.

Whether it has something to do with me or not, I'm not sure yet.

"Tiny, can I get another beer?" Breaker asks as he sits on the stool in front of where I've been standing.

"Sure," I murmur, turning to grab him one out of the cooler behind me and hand it to the guy.

"Thanks, babe." Grinning, Breaker takes the bottle out of my hand.

"Breaker, baby." I cringe at the squeal of the woman's voice who called Breaker's name from across the bar.

"Fuck," he mutters, his back tensing before he plasters a grin to his face and faces the woman. "Noémie, what are you doing here?"

"Chains called me. Said he needed to talk to me. I've missed you two guys, maybe the three of us can have some fun. We haven't in months" As her words hit my ears, it's as if a bullet has penetrated my heart.

"Chains, called you?" Breaker asks before I can.

"Yeah, said it was important that I come to the clubhouse," She giggles as she turns to me. "Can I get a margarita?"

Unable to speak, I nod and go about fixing the woman her drink.

"Don't go trying to start trouble, Noémie," Breaker says, his arm still around the woman.

"Who me? I never cause trouble you know that, baby," Noémie smirks.

"Bullshit, woman. Let me shoot Prez a text letting him know you're here," he mutters, reaching into his pocket but Noémie stops him.

"That's okay. I can find him," she smirks taking the glass I'd just put on the bar top.

Who the fuck is this woman? Better yet, why did Chains call her. Is he done with me already? He has to be. I mean look at this woman. She looks like a runway model whereas I'm barely tall enough to reach the bottom shelf with all the liquor on it.

"I don't think that's a good idea," Breaker says firmly glancing in my direction.

"Of course, it is. It wouldn't be if he hadn't called me here himself. But as it is Chains did," she argues and takes a sip of her drink. "Yum this is so good, for a stray you make a damn good drink," Noémie laughs.

"Fuck," Breaker grunts as I ball my hands into fists.

"I'm sorry but excuse me. Did you just call me a stray?" I snap, pissed she'd judge me for working behind the bar.

Wait, no, I'm pissed she's rubbing in the fact, Chains, called her here. More importantly, he'd find someone else before telling me he's done.

What else should I expect? He deserves something more than me. I'm nothing compared to this woman. But it doesn't mean I'm going to let her know this.

"Well, that is what you are. I mean no offense doll face, but there is no way any man in this building would go for a little girl like you unless it was for free pussy. I mean besides the long hair you have nothing to offer." Thanks for the confidence boost bitch.

"Noémie, I'd suggest you not insult Prez's ol' lady again," Breaker sneers, gripping the bitch's arm now rather than sitting with his arm around her waist.

"What?" she screeches. "You're Chains' ol' lady. Yeah fuckin' right. That man wouldn't settle for some little girl who looks like a bitch like you," she yells, cocking her hip as she crosses her arms over her chest.

"Evidently, he did, considering I'm the one he takes to bed every night," I state.

"Oh, honey just because he takes you to bed every night doesn't mean you're his ol' lady. Only that you're the pick of the month for now," she giggles.

Fury consumes me and I'm about ready to jump over the bar when the man himself makes his presence known. "What the fuckin' hell are you doing here, Noémie?" he demands.

"Baby, I'm here because you called me, remember?" the bitch says, sweetly, snatching her arm away from Breaker.

"I didn't fuckin' tell you to come here. I told your skank ass to wait at the bar for Tyres and Brake to get there and give them the information you had. Nowhere in our conversation did I invite you to the clubhouse," Chains sneers.

"It's been months since you fucked me, and I

figured you needed a load off. There's no way this little girl is giving you what I can," she whines, and I don't even hide the rolling of my eyes.

"Bitsy, come here," Chains commands.

Nodding, I make my way around the bar to do as he demanded. I may be upset but I'm not about to let it show right now. Not in front of this bitch or anyone else. That's one thing I learned from Rachel, and in our last conversation she reminded me of her motto. Show no weakness.

Once I'm in reaching distance, Chains reaches for me to pull me the rest of the way into his arms. Turning me so that my front is pressed against his, he leans forward to capture my mouth in a quick but commanding kiss.

Standing back to his full height, Chains turns his attention to the room. "I may not have had my ink put on my ol' lady yet nor have I given her her patch. But all the same, Tiny is my fuckin' ol lady. Mine. Does everyone understand?" he bellows into the room which has now gone deathly quiet.

"Prez, we all knew she was your ol' lady." Crash, one of the members of the club yells from across the room. Dee was sitting on his lap giving me a glare.

"I'm speaking to all the strays and hang arounds," Chains says.

"I'm sure they understand, Darren," I murmur for only him to hear.

"Good, because I won't allow any one and I mean no fuckin' body to disrespect you," he grinds out.

"Okay," I say as I meet his gaze taking in the fury swirling inside them.

Without another word, he nods and lifts his head to Tyres who I didn't even notice had joined our group. "Deal with this bitch for me and have Shock take over bartending for the night. Tiny's off," he states right before releasing his hold on me.

I'm about to tell him that I was fine working when I find myself being thrown over Chains' shoulder.

CHAPTER FIFTEEN

Chains

Mother fuckin' bitch thinks she can come into my clubhouse and disrespect my ol' lady, all because I quit givin' her my dick.

Fuck.

I'd seen the doubts start to seep into my woman's gaze from the camera in my office. Fuse, Tyres, and I had been going over some shit that he had seen on the video feed at the Delancy's when something on the screen next to the one we were looking at caught my attention.

I'd turned the volume to the monitor up to hear what was going on in the main room of the clubhouse, I turned my focus solely on what's going on with Tiny and those around her. It's not easy with the music being so loud but I made do.

She had been hurt by Noémie's words and probably with the way I've been acting recently.

Over the past month, I've been distracted with getting everything organized to take out the Delancys. I'd called Noémie when she'd texted me from the strip club she works at and overheard Delano talking to Parker. After telling the bitch to wait at the bar, in the French Quarter the club owns, until Tyres and Brake got there, I'd hung up.

Where Noémie thought I told her to come to the clubhouse is beyond me. Sure, Breaker and I use to double team her together, but I sure as fuck don't think she's a good enough lay for me to look the other way when it comes to my ol' lady.

That shit doesn't fly with me. Not everyone is the same and it ain't my business but when it comes to my relationship, I'm not about to throw it away or have Tiny look the other way. It's not how my dad raised me. Hell, it ain't how Ryder brought me up after my dad died.

It's time to show my Bitsy she means everything to me. I'd been waiting until I took out those fuckers to give her the cut, I'd ordered it weeks ago. It'd finally come in but until this mess was over with, I needed to make sure she was protected.

As of now, I don't give a rat's ass if Deanna sees it on my woman anymore or not. Tiny deserves to know what she means to me and not be hidden away in fear.

Bending forward, I throw Tiny onto the bed and climb over her until I have her caged between my arms.

"Seems we have a few things to get straight, baby," I growl as I meet her gaze.

"I highly doubt that. Seems to me things are quite clear," she whispers, quietly.

"Wanna expand on how things are so clear?" I demand.

"You may have said what you did out there as a saving face moment, but I know you don't really want me. Not really. I mean, how could you? Compared to Noémie and the other women who surround you, I'm nothing. I barely have tits or an ass. She's right I look like a little girl." Lifting a hand, I wipe the tears that fall from the corners of her eyes.

"Bitsy, didn't I tell you that I love you?" I ask, softly.

"Yes, but you could have changed your mind," she murmurs.

"That's not going to happen. Besides my sister, I've never told another woman I loved her. Not even Deanna." I say, honestly.

"Deanna?" she asks, her brow furrows in confusion.

"I'll explain things about her in a minute, baby. What you need to understand now, is that you are it for me. No one else is going to be able to do what you have." Leaning forward, I brush my lips against hers.

"What's that?"

"You own my fuckin' heart, baby, that's what you do."

"Then why have you been so distant from me. I mean besides here in this room. You've barely paid any attention to me." I knew I'd hurt her by ignoring her, but I was trying to get everything in order to take the Delancys out, sooner rather than later.

"Sloane, I know you've been around clubs and know that there are things I won't discuss with you. This is one of them. I will say this though, I didn't mean to hurt your feelings by ignoring you. I've been working on taking care of a problem the club's been dealing with for years and . . ."

"I don't need to know the details unless you want to tell me. But you also need to know, I don't need you to protect me from every little thing. I get the club has problems, I've heard bits and pieces to know it's some serious stuff. But I'm not weak and can help. Yes, am I terrified of going to town alone or being too close to people? Yes, I'm petrified to do either, however when you're around the feelings aren't so terrible. Knowing that I can come to you helps with my anxiety. So please just stop keeping me at arm's length out there. I can handle myself because I trust in you that if

I begin to fall you will be there to make sure I'm not hurt."

"Fuck, Bitsy," I say before capturing her mouth thrusting my tongue into hers as I move my hands between us and unbutton her jeans. After that little speech, I need to be balls deep inside of her more now than ever.

Without breaking our kiss, I slip Tiny's pants and underwear down in one swoop. Next, I unfasten and pull my jeans down just enough to release my dick from its confines. I quickly slide a finger through her slit to make sure she's ready for me. Finding what I want, I thrust all the way to the hilt making my woman scream my name.

Throwing Tiny's legs over my shoulders to get the angle I want; I deepen my thrusts as I fuck my woman with a ruthless speed. I take out all of my pent-up stress, that I'd been holding in, out on her body. I may have been fuckin' Tiny since we started but nothing like this.

Thrusting into Tiny's pussy, I break the kiss, panting for breath. Meeting her gaze, I thrust even harder into her.

Sweat begins to build on my forehead as my orgasm starts to build. At the same time, Tiny's nails sink into my back as her pussy begins to tighten around my dick.

"Fuck, Sloane. Come on my dick," I order knowing what being told what to do will do to her.

Screaming my name, she clamps down on my dick pulling my orgasm from me all at the same time. I roar her name as I spurt every last drop of my come into her.

"Darren," she murmurs, breathlessly and fuck if my dick doesn't twitch ready for another round.

"I fuckin' love you, Sloane. Don't you ever doubt that," I rasp before pulling out of her. Groaning I sit back on my still jean clad legs and stare down between us.

Fuck me, we didn't use a condom. "Uhh, baby, I never asked and it's pretty shitty to be asking now after being inside you, but are you on birth control?" I'm betting I already know the answer to that question; however, I need confirmation on it.

"Umm, I was on the shot for a while. But I haven't had one since being here and I was due for one right after I moved here," she says, drawing her bottom lip between her teeth.

"Damn, baby, don't do that. I'll end up fuckin' you all over again. You don't know what nibbling on your lip does to me." I groan as I stand up. "We have two options, Bitsy. Either go get a Plan B pill or we wait to see if you get pregnant. If we go get the pill, I won't be pissed. Just means you're not ready and we'll use condoms until we can get you on birth control. Now if you want to wait and see, then I don't want to use condoms anymore. Feeling your pussy bare felt too damn good to give up."

"Umm, I really like not having a barrier between us," she murmurs with a smile.

"Plan B?" I ask.

"I don't believe in it." Fuckin' hell. Can she get any more perfect for me than she already is?

CHAPTER SIXTEEN

Tiny

Holy mother of all flying monkeys in the sky.

This guy knows just how to make everything better. Okay I'll rephrase that. His dick makes everything better with blissful orgasms that relax me.

After the first one of the night, during our heart to heart, we stripped down completely. Pulling me with him, Chains drew a shower for us. He then proceeded to toy with my pussy and make me come twice before he took me against the shower wall.

Now lying in his arms, I feel lighter than I think I ever have, however, we still have a lot to talk about.

"Who's Deanna?" I ask, my fingers trailing designs along his muscular chest.

Sighing, Chains sits up and leans against the headboard. "Deanna was my best friend growing up. As we got older, I thought she was the one for me. I couldn't have been more wrong with that one."

"Right after high school, Deanna married the man who killed my parents. I wanted to rip his throat out when I realized that's who she was marrying. I'd started to make plans to rescue her from the life she was doomed for. However, she didn't want to be rescued. Deanna was power hungry and decided being Delano's queen she'd be able to do what she wanted."

"Hell, the bitchhonestly thought she could have me as her side piece. That didn't work out too well for her. After Delano found out her little plan, thanks to one of her supposed friends, he killed the informant right in front of Deanna to prove to her she wasn't to be with anyone but him. So she'd turned into not just a power hungry bitch, she became a psychopath killing people when she felt like it, stealing women and young girls off the streets to make them slaves in either one of her brothels or to be sold."

"Wow, that's just wow. I can't even think of the words to describe what I think of that," I say, sitting up to look at Chains.

"Nothing to say about it, Bitsy, the bitch is a fuckin' lunatic. Reason I didn't want her to see you is because I don't want her to do anything to you."

My heart skips a beat at his statement. Well more

along the lines of the torment that seems to be swirling in his gaze.

"Nothing is going to happen to me," I murmur, lifting a hand to touch the scruff on his face.

"You don't know that, Sloane," he mutters, closing his eyes for a brief moment. "My parents died at the hands of Deanna's husband. She's had years to learn from him. Fuck, in my opinion she's sicker than he is. I've seen what she does and it's not pretty."

"I can know that, you know why?"

"Why?" Meeting my gaze, Chains, seems to be getting agitated.

"Because I trust you, Chains. I'm not going to do anything without you and it's not like I leave the clubhouse except for that one time."

"That's going to change, baby, you should be going out, shopping, making friends, and what not," he argues.

"But I'm happy with the way things are now. If and when I'm ready to go out again, I know I can talk to you." Smiling, I straddle his hips. "Besides, I'm not going to let that bitch or anyone else win. Let the woman find out about me. I'm betting when she hears about me being your ol' lady she'll make a move which will leave you open to take her down if you want. And if it helps any, I'll pull the trigger."

"Fuckin' hell, Bitsy. Talkin' about you being bait isn't

something I'm willing to do. But have to say the thought of you with a gun in your hand is hot as fuck. Do you even know how to use a gun?" Grinning, I nod my head.

"Yep, I do. In fact, your sister and Rachel made a point of dragging me out of my room and to the shooting range to teach me. Evidently, I'm an excellent shot," I say confidently. What I don't say is how I'd envisioned the bullseye as the faces of the men who hurt me. From my father to Jackal and the nameless people on the streets who'd tried.

"Damn, tomorrow we're going to the range. I wanna see what you have," Chains declares, his hands moving up my legs to grip my waist.

Without any barriers between us, Chains' dick is pressed against my core.

"Darren," I moan, as Chains guides my movements over his shaft.

"You like that Sloane, my dick sliding between your pussy lips, rubbing against your clit. You're fuckin' soaking me already," he rasps, right before he stops me. "Wait. I wanna do something, baby." Sliding me off of him, I start to protest when he gets out of the bed.

I follow him with my gaze as he walks over to the closet and opens the door slightly. "I'm not fuckin' you again until you have this," he says, turning back to me after closing the closet with something clutched in his hand.

My breath catches when I realize exactly what Chains is holding.

"Stand up, Sloane," he commands.

Slowly, I crawl to the edge of the bed. My gaze stays locked with his, the entire time, as my heart pounds against my chest.

"Darren," I murmur when I'm standing directly in front of him.

"Bitsy, I claimed you as mine and I'm never letting you go," he growls as he puts the cut on my naked body.

Glancing down, tears well in my eyes. By him putting this on me means everything to me. He didn't just hand it to me. No, Chains showed me the importance of this by sliding it onto my body the first time himself.

"I love you," I whisper, reaching up on my tiptoes as I wrap my arms over his shoulders.

"Love you too, Sloane," he rasps, tilting his head down to meet me in the middle. Kissing me lightly, Chains lifts me up into his arms. His dick presses at my entrance when I wrap my legs around his waist. "Now, I'm gonna fuck you the rest of the night with you wearing my cut, baby."

"Hmmm, I like that idea," I giggle and sink down on to him.

"Good," he groans while laying me on the bed and rolling us until I'm on top of him. "Ride me, Sloane."

Smiling down at him, I begin to do as he commands. I ride him nice and slow teasing him, wanting to prolong our pleasure.

Feeling lighter than I ever have, I don't want it to end.

But you know what they say.

Nothing lasts forever.

CHAPTER SEVENTEEN

Chains

"Bitsy, did you fill out the application for school yet?" I ask Tiny during breakfast as I stare at her. I can't seem to take my gaze off of her. Seeing her in my property cut does something to me. Last night I fucked her every way possible while she wore it over her naked tits.

Fuck. I'd even had her pose for me in the middle of the bed this morning in nothing but her cut and panties so I could take a picture.

It's now the background on my phone.

"I did," she says, quietly glancing around the table. Seeing that my brothers were paying attention, she lowers her head in embarrassment.

"Tiny, don't be ashamed of wanting to go to school." Axel says, from a few chairs down.

"Yeah, there's nothing to be ashamed about," Breaker grins.

"Shit, if it makes you feel better, I'll apply and do it with you," Speed states from the other end of the table. He's one of our newest brothers but he's damn good at covering our backs when needed. We don't call him Speed for nothing. The man is constantly going and has a lead foot.

"Thank you," Tiny says, but the blush still tints her cheeks.

"Baby, look at me," I command as I reach over to hold her hand. "You have nothing to be nervous about nor ashamed of. You're smart and you can do this. When it comes time for school, remember you have all of our support."

"Damn right," Tyres grunts from where he's sitting on the other side of me. "Tiny, you're not just Prez's ol' lady. You're family to us. The moment you walked into the clubhouse with Shadow you became like a little sister to all of us. Well, except your ol' man here," he grins.

As I open my mouth to respond, the front door to the clubhouse is thrown open and one of our prospects, Shock, rushes into the room.

"Prez, there's a box at the gate you need to see," he

says in a rush.

Tensing, I stand up. "Why didn't you just bring the box up here?" I demand.

"Couldn't lift it by myself," Shock responds.

Nodding, I look down at Tiny. "Stay in here, okay?"

"Okay. I'll just go start cleaning up breakfast," she says, quietly.

"Have the strays do it. You have enough other stuff on your plate to do," I suggest, knowing she'd planned to do inventory of the bar today.

Nodding, she stands up and I lean down to give her a quick kiss before heading out the door.

Making my way to the gate, I take in the size of the box with narrowed eyes.

"What the fuck?" Breaker snarls as he walks next to me.

"I'm not liking this," Tyres mutters.

"Me either," I say in agreement.

The moment I get to the box, I notice an envelope taped to the top. Snatching the damn thing off the box, I open it up to read what it says.

I hope you enjoyed the show the other night, sweetheart, because when I get my hands on that bitch, I'll do the same to her. Remember when I said if I couldn't have you no one can? Well that goes for this little girl as well. As they say misery loves company and you my sweetheart are my company, Darren and I'll never let you be. Not even in death will that happen. Here's a gift for you. I hope you like it because she was outstanding.

Deanna

Fury consumes me as I reread the letter.

"Open the box," I snarl, dreading what we're about to find in it.

Pitch Black pulls his knife out and cuts the tape away. Flipping the flaps to the side, we all get a good look at what's inside. Curses surround me as I take in the sight of the poor girl we'd seen on the live feed Fuse had brought to my attention yesterday. He'd come to me when he'd noticed Deanna seemed to look directly into the camera we'd had placed in their house almost a year ago.

Bruises from the beating she received cover her entire body. Blood smeared across her pale skin from the slashes she'd taken. Visions of the footage yesterday fill my mind, her muted screams.

We'd failed this girl, because of the situation being caused in the bar with Noémie. I'd been blinded by my girl being hurt that we didn't get to save this one. If only we'd acted last night, she might still be alive.

"Fuck," I snarl, closing my eyes in frustration. Then it hits me. She'd set it up. That fuckin' bitch sent Noémie here.

Turning on my heel I head toward the clubhouse, "Church now. Shock and Crank get this out of here.

We don't need the police coming thinking we had anything to do with this shit. Put her somewhere her body will be found though. When you're done with that go pick-up Noémie."

"You got it, Prez," Shock says.

"Why do they need to get that bitch?" Brake asks.

"Because that fuckin' bitch was part of Deanna's plan," I growl, throwing the door open. It bangs against the wall and out of the corner of my eye I see Tiny jump.

"Bitsy, need you to stay inside no matter what needs to be done. You need something outside, you get a prospect," I say, not stopping on the way to the room we all meet for church.

The moment we're all in the room I take my seat and grab a cigarette out of the pack I keep in here for when I really need one.

"What did the letter say?" Tyres asks doing the same as me. Neither of us smoke often but when bad shit's surrounding us, we do. Actually, several of us do. Some prefer weed to cigarettes so the room becomes a mixture of smoke.

"That girl was a pawn to show us that Deanna knows we have eyes on them. She also states that Tiny is next," I sneer, slamming a fist on the large oak table my grandfather built himself. "Crazy, stupid bitch seems to have completely gone insane."

"What do you want to do?" Ryder growls.

"I say it's time we send her and the rest of them through the inferno of hell," I declare.

Each of my brothers nod their heads in agreement.

"Burn the motherfuckers to the ground," Breaker sneers.

Nodding my head, I light another cigarette as we start to go over the last bit of details for what we'd been planning to do.

Tonight, the sky will glow bright with the fires coming for those who fucked with us.

CHAPTER EIGHTEEN

Tiny

Something bad is going on and I'm starting to worry. When all the club members went into the room they hold church in, I knew whatever had been in that box Shock had mentioned, it wasn't good.

Trying to take my mind off what's going on, I busy myself with cleaning the bar. I move all of the liquor bottles and glasses in order to wipe the shelves down. Unable to get the top shelves I climb up onto the counter behind the bar to reach the top.

In the middle of wiping the top shelf the front door opens, bringing with it the light from the afternoon sun. My jaw nearly drops to the floor at seeing the group of people who just stepped into the clubhouse.

Distracted by the intrusion, I lose my footing and

fall from the counter landing on my butt. Worst of it was the fact I ended up bringing the bar down with me. Glasses crash around me and liquor bottles break.

"Shit," I groan, laying against the cold floor in somewhat of a daze at the same time my name is yelled by several people.

"What the fuck is going on in here?" Chains demands, though I can't see him from behind the bar. I can imagine his gaze narrowing at the fact church was interrupted. "What the . . . shit. Bitsy."

"Don't move," Raven orders. I didn't even realize she was next to me.

"Someone want to tell me why you all are here?" Chains mutters as he makes it to my side. His question directed at not only Raven but his sister and several members from the Devil's Riot MC that are with them.

"Figured it was time for a visit with my big brother," Vi says, causing me to giggle which turns into a groan due to the pain in my rear.

"Bitsy, what the hell happened?" Chains asks, softly.

Focusing my gaze on him, I try to smile through the pain. "I slipped."

"You slipped? Baby, seriously you slip, and I come in here to find you laid out on the floor with glass all around you."

"Sorry it's our fault, we startled her without meaning to when we came in." I hear Stoney say.

With gentle movements, Chains lifts me into his arms and stands to his full height. He sits me on the top of the bar as Pipe comes around the bar to make sure I'm okay along with Ranger.

"I'm okay," I mutter, holding my hands up to stop everyone hovering anymore.

"Good, now tell me how the hell you slipped," Chains grumbles.

"I was cleaning the top shelves when the door opened, distracting me and I lost my footing. I'm sorry I broke all the glasses," I say, lowering my head.

I'm sure he's probably pissed as hell at me for breaking everything.

"Look at me, Sloane." Cupping the side of my face, Chains guides my movements until I'm meeting his gaze. "I'm not worried about the fuckin' glasses or liquor that shit's replaceable. You're not, baby. Next time you want to clean the top shelves, a prospect will handle it for you. No more climbing shit. Got me?"

I nod my head in response.

"Well I'm glad to see I was right," Victoria says, breaking the moment between Chains and myself.

"Wanna tell me what you all are doing here?" Chains asks, his gaze moving from each person who had come in with his sister.

"I called Mom about something and she told me

you guys might need some help," Raven says, a broom already in her hand.

"We're family, Chains. I'm not about to let you do anything without backup," Victoria says.

"Exactly what your sister said. Besides, we all missed munchkin here," Stoney says, glancing between Chains and I, causing me to grin when he notices the cut I'm wearing. "Good to finally see you happy, Tiny."

"Thank you, Stoney. Hey everyone. I'd offer you something to drink but it seems I've broken all of the glasses out here," I state jokingly trying to lighten the mood.

Chuckles fill the room, but Chains doesn't find it amusing.

"I promise no more climbing," I murmur to him.

Stepping closer to me, Chains leans forward. "You better not or I'll make sure you don't sit for a week," he whispers before kissing me.

"Excuse me, can we have some time with our girl here please?" I giggle at the voice because the guys don't know what they're in for with her being here. I'm honestly shocked she'd come.

"Kenny," I say excitedly, sliding off the bar top with Chains help and moving to hug the woman. I'd become friends with her before I'd met Rachel and they both became two of my best friends.

"Tiny, look at you. Finally opening that shell and I can see why. Nice," she says winking at me.

"Watch it, woman," Horse mutters behind her.

"I will watch it. Maybe me and Tiny here can compare notes," she says.

"Make sure I'm not there for that talk," Victoria mutters.

"Same here. I'm sorry but I'm married to Horse's dad, I don't want or need the visual of what he's packing because I'm pretty sure I already know," Rachel groans.

"That's because he looks just like him," Kenny states, moving her hands between the two men.

"Jesus Christ, is it always like this?" Breaker asks, looking horrified.

"Yep," Tracker groans. "Just wait it gets worse. Though Tiny's never partaken, these women when they drink are nuts."

"Hey, you like it when I'm drunk," Victoria smirks.

"Alright, that's enough of that shit. I do not want to hear anything about my sister's sex life," Chains mutters.

"Where are all the kids?" I ask.

"They're back home. The only reason I left Jamie was because of the feeling I'd had when Raven told me about her mom's vision." At the mention of Ela, I smile. She is one of the nicest women I've ever met, and I sometimes wish I had a mom like her.

She hadn't been around much recently due to her sister being sick. but Ela texts me often with inspirational quotes.

Right before I was about to respond, Shock and Crank came in the front door, both looking grim.

"Everything go okay?" Chains asks them and they both nodded as they looked around the room.

"Yeah, got it handled; however, we couldn't find her," Shock says.

"Shit," Chains says.

"Got what handled?" Victoria asks at the same time.

"Club business Vi," Chains mutters. "Look it's cool you all came down and we'll be more than happy to have you all here to help but, Victoria, You and Raven are out of this. I don't need the stress of it."

"Not happening, Chains," Vi says sarcastically as she folds her arms over her chest.

"Victoria, you finally have everything you deserve, don't go down this road again. You're retired from the bullshit," Ryder proclaims as he moves to stand next to Chains.

"Uncle Ryder," Vi says, enthusiastically.

"Hey, sweetheart," Ryder murmurs to his niece.

"Look, Vi, why don't you do me a solid and hang

out with the women while the clubs discuss the situation."

Before anything else can be said an explosion rocks the building and the lights go out leaving us in complete darkness. It might be daylight outside but in here without light it's a blackout.

"Chains," I yell, trying to find him in the dark.

Through the commotion I can hear him calling out for me as well as directing orders to his brothers.

A cloth covers my mouth and nose as an arm wraps around my waist. "Easy, bitch," I would've cringed at the voice if I didn't faint in their hold.

CHAPTER NINETEEN

Chains

I'm gonna kill the motherfucker who threw an explosive at the clubhouse. But I already know.

"Fuckin' Deanna," I snarl as everyone stands outside. Well almost everyone.

Somehow Tiny was taken within the short period of time it took us to get everyone out of the clubhouse.

"Don't worry brother we'll get her back," Tyres says.

"You're fuckin' right I will. Deanna fucked up." I sneer, and head for my bike. My brothers behind me. We don't need to go over the plan anymore. The plan has changed.

"Chains," Vi yells. Turning my head, I see her approaching me with a look of determination.

"Don't have time, Vi," I mutter.

"Let me help. I know you don't want me to, but you also know I can get in and out of somewhere without being detected," she argues.

"Not this time, Vi. You want to help, can you handle getting this stuff organized for me. See what all the damage is and a list of what needs to be fixed," I state.

"Fine," she huffs. "But at least let Tracker's club help you."

"Alright," I grumble, knowing having them with us would be helpful.

"Thank you, stay safe and bring my sister in-law home," Vi grins.

"I plan on it." Straddling my bike, I watch my sister run over to Tracker. Nodding he and the rest of the Devil's Riot move to their own bikes.

When I get Tiny back, I'm investing in a monitor for the front gate. One that lets the club know when someone comes through. Better yet a sensor for anytime the gate opens. This shit won't be happening again.

Starting my bike, I glance in my brothers' direction getting nods from each of them letting me know they're ready.

Pulling out of the parking lot of the clubhouse, I turn in the direction of the one place I'm willing to bet

Deanna would take my woman. The one place where everything started with us a long time ago.

Pushing my girl to the limit, I head to the shack near the house I grew up in. The place where I found Deanna one day when we were just kids. She'd been lost in the woods and found the shack I'd claimed as my *Fort*.

By the time I make it to the tree line, my rage is at its limit.

"Prez, you sure this is where they'd have brought her?" Brake asks.

"Oh, I'm sure and I'm willing to bet she did this without Delano," I sneer.

"What can we do to help?" Stoney asks.

"Watch your step and follow me. If you see any men in suits, shoot 'em. Anyone who didn't come into these woods with us and Tiny is fair game. This is private property and no one should be on this land besides the club," I declare and Stoney grins.

"My kinda fun here, alright let's go have some target practice," the man says nodding his head.

Fuckin' hell you find allies in the strangest ways. Having my sister become his VP's ol' lady worked out in both our favors. Doesn't mean I didn't look into them when I found out about her being with the dude.

Shaking my head, I focus on one thing. Getting my ol'

lady back from the psycho-bitch from hell. With each step I take I force the memories of this place out of my head. No longer will they ever hold any meaning to me but hatred because of Deanna. She ruined everything when it came to this place. It used to be mine and then I met her. I thought she was everything the way she'd smile so bright.

I barely register the shot that hits me. Reaching up to my shoulder, I pull my hand back to find some fucker has shot me.

Not letting it stop me, I keep walking toward the shack that's now in my sight.

More shots are taken as people start to yell around me; however, I keep my focus solely on making my way toward my woman.

"I knew you'd know where to find me, sweetheart," Deanna giggles from the entrance.

"You crossed a line, Dea. This time you've gone too far going after my ol' lady," I sneer.

"Gone too far? I highly doubt that," she laughs, stepping closer to me.

"Where's Tiny?" I demand.

"Don't worry about that little girl. I told you I wasn't giving you up and I meant it. I've lived in hell and I won't do it alone," she says.

"Dea, quit this shit now." My fingers itch to grab my gun and pull the trigger that would end her. I don't normally condone harming women, but Deanna is far from being classified as a woman in my book.

"I don't think so, you see the day I saw you two in the French Quarter, I knew she was different. The way you looked at her told me everything I needed to know. She was special and going to take my place in your heart," she rambles on, her eyes filling with tears.

"You were never in my heart the way she is," I growl.

"That's a lie and you know it," she screams. "But that's okay because now I won't have to worry about it anymore." The smirk that crosses her face is one that could be called demonic when she raises a gun and pulls the trigger before I can react.

"No." I hear Tiny scream as I stagger backwards into a tree and slide down.

My vision blurs and I swear I start to hallucinate when I hear more gunshots. Deanna's body drops.

"Chains, please stay with me," Tiny cries as she looks down at me. Her hands press against my chest.

"I love you," I cough out.

"I love you too, Darren. Stay with me. I can't lose you. Please. Please. Just hold on," she sobs.

"You can't lose what will always be with you."

Shouts come from all directions as Tiny screams for help.

"Promise me, Bitsy, that you'll go on living for me," I murmur, reaching up to touch her.

"I can't, Darren. I can't do that. I need you." My head becomes lighter and I have a hard time keeping my eyes open.

"We're losing him," Pipe yells and my body is being hoisted.

The last thing I hear are my woman's screams of agony.

EPILOGUE

Tiny

The day Deanna took me I swear it was one of the worst days of my life. I never expected things to end this way.

After Deanna shot Chains, I'd ended her by using the very same gun to kill her. Just because I'm small doesn't mean I'm not able to handle my own. I know a thing or two. And given the fact I was facing losing the love of my life, I wanted Deanna's blood.

Taking her by surprise I'd tackled her to the ground and snatched the gun from her hands. Directly after, I'd shot her square between the eyes before dropping the gun to the ground.

My heart was ripped out of my chest.

If not for Raven and Victoria showing up when they did with an SUV, you might as well have put a bullet in my chest as well.

By the time we arrived at the hospital, they were waiting at the entrance with a gurney to take Chains to the back. I don't know how they knew and didn't care. From what the doctors said he coded on the table several times while they tried to save him.

It took all my strength to keep moving through the days. The guys from the club have been supportive. Even the guys from the Devil's Riot MC. But they had to get back to their club house; however, they did ask if the club would look out for someone who was planning to move out this way for them. Victoria had been apprehensive about leaving yet she couldn't be away from her son any longer. I didn't blame her. I'd be the same way.

At the time when they asked, I didn't care. Hell, I still don't, but they're supposed to be arriving any day now.

It's been two weeks since that dreadful day and I've barely slept or eaten. Breaker, Brake, and Tyres have constantly taken turns sitting with me.

"Tiny, I'm gonna go get a coffee, you want something," Breaker asks as he stands stretching from being in the stiff chair for so long.

Shaking my head, I don't say anything as I continue to stare into the blackhole that seems to be taking over my life.

Sighing, Breaker kneels in front of me. "It's gonna be okay, I promise you," he murmurs.

Nodding, I do my best to keep the tears at bay. It's hard to do when the only comfort you have is the steady beating coming from a monitor.

"I'll be right back," he says as he stands back up.

The door closes quietly behind him leaving me alone in the sterile room with the man who holds my heart.

Over the past two weeks it's been a waiting game. At first after they stopped the bleeding, pulled the bullet out and fixed the artery that had been nicked no one thought he'd make it. Chains spent the last two weeks in an induced coma. The doctor said with each day that he makes it through is a good sign.

Yesterday they'd started to reduce his medication that keeps him in the coma.

"Come on, Darren. I need you to wake up," I murmur.

"Bitsy." I jump at the sound of his voice. My gaze shoots to his and I swear my heart nearly comes out of my chest.

"Oh God, Darren. I thought I'd lost you," I cry, kissing his hand that I'd been holding this entire time.

"You can't get rid of me that easily," he croaks, and I release his hand to press the nurse's button at the same time grabbing the small cup of water sitting on the table next to me.

Opening a straw that was sitting next to it, I place the thing in the water and lift it up for Chains to sip from.

When he's done, I put it back on the table and take his hand back in mine. "God, you had me scared out of my mind," I whisper.

"There's no way I could leave you, Bitsy," he murmurs. "Told you, you hold my heart. I'm not going anywhere."

"You better not. I don't want to live without you." I say, tears falling down my cheeks.

"Good, because when I get out of here, I'm puttin' my ring on your finger. You're stuck with me, Bitsy," he declares before letting his eyelashes flutter back down and drifts off back to sleep. At least this time when he closes his eyes, I know he'll be okay.

Standing up, I lean over him and press my lips to his. "Rest for now. Know that I'm here and nothing will happen to you. Trust me, Chains, the way I do in you. And yes, I'll marry you even if that was a crappy proposal," I murmur, knowing I'm the only one who can hear.

I only hope when he gets out of here that we can have a little bit of peace for a while.

The End For Now

Dear Readers,

Thank you so much for taking the time to read Chains' Trust. For those of you who have stuck with me since my first series Devil's Riot MC, thank you. This has been one crazy year so far and it's only going to get crazier. From the DRMC to the Dark Lullabies series. Then we have the RBMC (Elizabeth City Charter) and now the Inferno's Clutch MC.

Between all of the series' I'm working on, you'll have your hands full when it comes to these men and women as they find their way. Oh and let's not forget all the new character you've yet to meet.

Next up in the series is Breaker's Fuse. Will he be able to keep his cool when it comes time to or will he explode? Remember you can always reach out to me. You guys rock and I can't thank you enough for being a part of this ride with me.

Sincerely,
E.C.

Now here's some good news for you all if you think my Chains and Tiny's story is over. Think again. They will be back, and the danger will surround them.

Will Tiny be able to hold out hope when things come to light?

Find out this January in Tiny's Hope.

AVAILABLE NOW

By: E.C. Land

Devil's Riot MC Series

Horse's Bride

Thorn's Revenge

Twister's Survival

Reclaimed Boxset

Cleo's Rage

Connors' Devils

Hades Pain

Badger's Claim

Burner's Absolution

Devil's Riot MC Originals

Stoney's Property

Owning Victoria

Blaze's Mark

Dark Lullabies
A Demon's Bliss

Royal Bastards MC (Elizabeth City Charter)
Cyclone of Chaos

Anthologies
Guns Blazing
Rocked to the Core
Twisted Steel

COMING SOON
By: E.C. Land

Devil's Riot MC Originals
Taming Coyote
Luna's Shadow
Choosing Nerd
Carrying Blaze's Mark
Ranger's Fury
Neo's Strength

Dark Lullabies
A Demon's Soul
A Demon's Song

Inferno's Clutch MC
Breaker's Fuse
Ryder's Rush
Axel's Promise

Tiny's Hope
Fated for Pitch Black

Royal Bastards MC (Elizabeth City Charter)
Spiral of Chaos

Anthologies
Remembering Ryan
The Elites
Twisted Steel: Second Edition

Haven't read the Devil's Riot MC yet and want to know how their connected to the Inferno's Clutch MC? Check out Owning Victoria.

Prologue

Victoria
Two years ago

Running from the only home I've ever known is a scary thing, especially considering I grew up a spoiled little rich girl, as most people would say. Then again, nobody really knows what kind of life I've lived.

It's not always easy being the daughter of one of the most powerful men in the state. Nor is it best to deal with a mother who forces you to act perfect. Between the two of them, they created the person I am— a prim and proper lady who knows her place.

Or so they think.

On the outside, I gave them what they wanted to see while inside my head I was dying with each day that has gone by since the moment I turned fourteen. That was a little over four years ago, and the time is almost up. Tomorrow, I'm supposed to agree to a marriage I want nothing to do with in front of hundreds of people. All thanks to an arranged marriage my father and his made.

I've met the man I'm to vow my entire life to. I don't think my parents care that the man I'm supposed to marry will end up killing me. He's vile and would prefer a slave who will lay on her back rather than a wife to devote love to.

Every time I've raised my thoughts and concerns about this, I ended up spending the night in the cellar. Worse than that, my mother has been determined I am to be a size zero instead of the nine that I am. So, unless it's a handful of kale and spinach, I've barely eaten in a month.

I needed to get away.

That's why I'd packed a bag with the bare minimum items. I didn't need anything really but a few changes of clothes, a stash of money I kept hidden away and the little box my grandmother gave me. It contained pictures of her and I along with the pearls she'd given me before she passed.

Tonight, I made my move. I waited for my parents to go to bed. By the time the clock struck three a.m., I decided to say screw it and take my chances.

Slinking out the door to my room with my backpack on, I stuck to the shadows of the hallway and quietly made my way to my exit. The closer I got, I heard moans and groans.

Gross.

I might be a virgin, but I'm not naïve. I know what those sounds are. I shudder at the thought of my parents having sex. How two people who are as poisonous as them could have sex with each other is beyond me. My grandmother told me when I become intimate with someone, it should be with love and nothing else.

I made it to the door just as my mother's screams met my ears. I stilled as she called my soon-to-be-husband's name instead of my fathers'. Two different grunts can be heard as she goes silent.

Oh God, nausea churns my stomach. This is the life my parents want for me— one filled with deceit and despair.

Yeah, no, I'm good.

"Parker, it will be nice to have you around more," my mother purrs as I open the front door enough to fit through. I don't want to hear any more of this.

"That it will. I'll be more than happy to oblige you once your daughter is mine." Parker's chuckles send a horrifying chill down my spine.

Not going to happen, buddy.

I refuse to be with him.

I hold my breath as I pull the door closed behind me, hoping to God they don't hear the click of the door. I don't need them to catch me now. I'm too close to being home free of this insanity. Who wants to live like this?

Not me, that's for sure.

I want my freedom to do as I please. To love who I want. Be who I want and never have to worry what I am to those around me.

Making my way down the road, I get far enough away from the house and use my phone one last time to call the only friend I've ever known.

Raven.

Thankfully, she knew I would be calling.

"I see you. Just keep coming a little further and you'll see the car. Hurry up, though, we don't know how long it will take them to realize you're gone," she says before hanging up.

Nodding to myself, I pull the phone from my ear and throw it to the side. I won't be needing that one anymore. Raven has my new one.

Soon as I get to Raven's car, she starts the engine.

"Come on, babe, we gotta get some road between us and them," she states as I open the door and throw my stuff in the back and climb in.

"Yeah, I know we do," I mutter as I fasten my seat belt.

Raven wasted no time in getting us out of there either. Within thirty minutes, she's pulling onto I-20 heading east.

"Where are we headed?" I ask nervously. We'd never discussed where we'd go from here.

"Heading to Stonewall Mills, Virginia," she murmurs.

Stonewall Mills, interesting name.

Now, let's just hope my parents or Parker never find me there.

BE SURE TO FOLLOW OR STALK ME!

Goodreads
Bookbub
DRMC BABES
Instagram
Author Page

Printed in Great Britain
by Amazon